Mexico

www.stickingplacebooks.com

ISBN 978-1-942782-69-8

Mexico

The Aztec Account
of the Conquest

A screenplay by
Werner Herzog

Sticking Place Books
New York

The conquest of Mexico seen from the perspective of the Aztecs was a film project from the 1990s that never materialized because production costs would have been prohibitively high. Today, even though many of the locations and battle scenes could be done digitally, it would still require the budget of a huge Hollywood movie. This kind of budget I would be able to raise only if my last film grossed a few hundred million dollars at the domestic US box office. Such is the Iron Law of the industry.

But none of my films has grossed that much, and I felt that this screenplay has literary merit in its own right. I always wanted to develop screenplays as an independent form of literature. One normally would not publish a document like this before it is made into a film, but in this case the Iron Law still stands in my way.

I have spent not one sleepless night over the fact that I could not realize this project. Instead of waiting anxiously for years, I simply continued working, and since writing *Mexico* must have made more than thirty films.

Werner Herzog
Los Angeles, January 2024

GENERAL REMARKS

History and Story
For the sake of a motion picture story, the screenplay has to depart at times from historical exactness. Nezahualpilli, one of the protagonists, actually died two years prior to the arrival of Cortés. He did bet his kingdom against a turkey, but this referred to an earlier Spanish expedition. Malinche had not learned Spanish from Aguilar; initially she translated Nahuatl, the Aztec language, into a Mayan dialect which Aguilar understood and in turn translated into Spanish. The scene with Cortés demanding gold and drawing a line with his sword around the walls of a room never happened as depicted here. The incident really took place during the conquest of Peru, and involved Atahualpa and Pizarro.

Language
Since the Aztecs as "we" are our point-of-view characters, they will speak English. The Spaniards, "extraterrestrials," the "aliens," will speak Spanish. La Malinche is the translator throughout, but quite often she departs from her task and takes affairs into her own hands.

Names
There is a confusing variety of spellings of the name Motecuhzoma, this apparently being the most correct way to spell it. The Spaniards simply distorted his name into "Montezuma." La Malinche was called Marina by the Spaniards, or Doña Marina.

Her real name seems to have been Malinali, and Malinche actually means "master of Malinali," but since her name is so well established we call her Malinche, and refer to Cortés sometimes as Master of Malinche.

In the Aztec language, "x" is pronounced *sh*. In order to avoid confusion for modern viewers, "Mexico" should be pronounced in our customary way. Historically, Aztecs would refer to themselves as Mexicans, but most of the time we will avoid that reference.

Although the capital city was called Tenochtitlan, we will use more frequently the alternative name, "City of Mexico."

Stylistic Approach

Bold, imaginative. The Spanish completely leveled and obliterated Tenochtitlan, which originally appeared to them as an astonishing city of marvels, so all current theories concerning how it looked are at least part speculation. Most of the exterior images of the city will be realized through a variety of visual effects. Vast crowds of people (or fleets of dugout canoes) will be enormously enlarged by way of computer animation, with other effects achieved via an array of more conventional, less costly techniques (matte paintings, back projections, models, etc.).

The effects created will be stylized, rather than attempting to be purely realistic. The entire Aztec world will be stylized through acting, dialogue, costumes and props. This stylization of their strange world will succeed only if all the elements are equally stylized.

Although there will be a few instances in which we will recreate the authentic ancient music of the Aztecs (conch, rattles, whistles and drums), the musical score shall be contemporary film music, which transports the greatest emotions.

CAST OF CHARACTERS

MOTECUHZOMA
Around forty years old, tall, slender, dignified. Reserved demeanor, laconic, taciturn during his last days. Elected to head the royal realm in preference to his older brothers fifteen years before Cortés' arrival, he was distinguished by his superior qualities as both soldier and priest. A tender, low voice. Often indecisive, troubled, wavering between exaltation and despair. An aura of tragedy and drama around him.

CORTÉS
Hernán Cortés, in his mid-thirties, surprisingly young for a man of such momentous historical impact. A genius of deception and intrigue, masterful in diplomacy and leadership. Quick intelligence; shrewd, polite, bold and undeterred even amid the most adverse circumstances. Slight limp from his youth (in an attempt to climb into the bedroom of his lover, he fell from a wall). The enraged husband of his lady left a scar on Hernán's face with a sword. Even in his most casual moments he radiates authority. There is a vehemence beneath his guise of good manners. He is the most elegant of villains.

MALINCHE
Early twenties, interpreter for Cortés. She was an Aztec slave who came into Cortés' possession soon after his landing in the Yucatan. Historical sources describe her as highly intelligent and as beautiful as a goddess. She became Cortés' mistress and remains completely devoted and faithful to him. Horrible events in her childhood have turned her against her own countrymen. Her apparent hardness is betrayed by a deep vulnerability.

CUITLAHUAC
Motecuhzoma's older brother. More determined than the Mexican sovereign, and prudent. A good warrior. There is tension between his noble character and his simmering resentment for having been bypassed as ruler.

CUAUHTEMOC

Motecuhzoma's nephew. Early twenties, heroic, young, audacious. Fiercely opposed to the viewpoint of the Emperor, who, until the end, somehow believes the Spaniards are gods. Cuauhtemoc will become the last Aztec emperor. He defies death with intrepid resolution.

KEEPER OF THE HOUSE OF DARKNESS

Most prominent of the elite dignitaries. Late fifties, stern countenance. An advisor to Motecuhzoma who carries out important missions.

NEZAHUALPILLI

Old, white-haired, highly respected, no longer capable of fear. The subjugated King of Texcoco is the most clairvoyant and outspoken opponent of the Spanish conquistadors. With absolute certainty he is convinced that the Spaniards have come to destroy Mexico and all its Indian nations.

MALINCHE' S MOTHER

Early fifties, grey hair. In her youth, she must have been as beautiful as her daughter.

PEDRO DE ALVARADO

Early thirties. He's as wicked as he is handsome. Long blond hair, so blond that the Aztecs call him Tonatiuh, the Sun. During the absence of Cortés, he orders the massacre at the Great Temple. During the Night of Sorrows, Alvarado becomes famous for his desperate vault to safety across a breach in the causeway.

GERONIMO DE AGUILAR

Shipwrecked during an early Spanish expedition, he was held as a slave by the Mayans for many years. He has adopted indigenous customs and wears only a loincloth. Isolated and lonesome; he drowns during the Night of Sorrows.

BERNAL DIAZ
Young infantryman, boyish, innocent. Plants the first orange trees in the New World (and later becomes the most important chronicler of the conquest).

FATHER OLMEDO
Franciscan monk. Zealous, inspired by his mission to wean the natives from their heathenly abominations. Rotund; has difficulties when climbing at higher altitudes.

OKELLO
Spanish slave, the only black man in the Spanish expedition. The Aztecs marvel at him as the Eclipsed Sun. Young, tall, almost princely.

VISIONS. THE OMEN.

First, just a tone, endless and lamenting. Is it a flute? A human voice? Then an image flickers from the darkness: a vast landscape, utterly unreal, with tongues of fire flaring across the huge sky above. Now the flaming portent begins to bleed fire, drop by drop, like a deep wound in the sky.

Then a distant city, burning: indistinct, mysterious. Columns of fire and black smoke rise diagonally with an awful lethargy, like lazy beasts sluggishly rolling around. In the foreground, vague human figures emerge, a relentless procession of half-starved refugees fleeing the infernal city.

CLOSE-UP: THE JOYFUL FACE OF A SMALL LAUGHING CHILD APPEARS.

The child is being carried on his father's shoulders, a man nearly starved to death, staggering forward with the soundlessly weeping people. The little one is too young to understand, laughing and rejoicing because it's so much fun to be on daddy's shoulders, as his face passes toward the light of dawn. And the light is pale, and strange.

INTERIOR. MOTECUHZOMA'S PALACE. NIGHT.

CLOSE-UP: A SLEEPING MAN, FOR AN INSTANT.

Suddenly the face shoots up in horror, waking in a terrified flash, the dark knowing eyes glaring at us dead on. Sharp features, blue-black hair, bronze skin, a hint of a sparse moustache and beard on lip and chin. This is Motecuhzoma.

MOTECUHZOMA

Guards!

Hustling footsteps, the hissing sound of a moving flame, then a fiery torch leaps into frame as a young guard bows to Motecuhzoma. Their eyes meet.

CLOSE-UP: THE GUARD'S AGITATED EYES GAZE FORTH, THEN SHIFT DOWN.

Forbidden from looking at his lord, he abruptly turns his face away.

> GUARD
> My lord?

> MOTECUHZOMA
> Attend.

Now Motecuhzoma's voice lowers, urgently.

> MOTECUHZOMA
> Light the Great Hall – *silently*, do not wake
> the palace. Assemble the Crown Council
> at once. Wake my brother, Cuitlahuac, and
> King Nezahualpilli. Wake my nephew,
> Cuauhtemoc, and the Keeper of the House
> of Darkness. Rouse them – wake them all,
> and alert them. And find my magician.

Seven guardsmen fly off in all directions. As sparks from their torches linger in the air we glimpse the simple, flower-strewn room, and solitary Motecuhzoma.

INTERIOR. THRONE ROOM IN PALACE. NIGHT.

The chamber is suffused with the warm glow of the torches. Slightly elevated, Motecuhzoma sits on a simple wicker throne, his cowering body wrapped in a spectacular blue and green cloak of glittering feathers, with gold sandals on his feet. Seated on mats in a semi-circle before him are the members of the Crown Council, a lone gap amid them.

Embarrassed, Cuitlahuac rushes in late, escorted by breathless guards, tossing aside his dazzling feathered cloak for one of rough maguey fibers that is placed over his shoulders.

He removes his sandals, touches the ground with his hand and kisses his fingers, then takes a seat on the mat with his barefoot peers, who also wear their burlap-like cloaks with an august dignity.

CLOSE-UPS: CUITLAHUAC, CUAUHTEMOC, NEZAHUALPILLI, THE IMPERIAL MAGICIAN, AND THE KEEPER OF THE HOUSE OF DARKNESS.

MOTECUHZOMA
I had a dream. I saw our lake boiling and
foaming and rising in rage, destroying all
the houses along our shores. And I saw our
City of Mexico in flames, and kings fleeing
to the hills, and a child being saved. I saw
him laughing.

MAGICIAN
My lord, there have been so many evil
omens this year, and so many of late. Like
the three-tailed comet that came at midday,
always at midday, and always stayed –

KEEPER
Your people are so terrified –

CUITLAHUAC
– that they can't *pray* any more. Everyone
is *trembling*. Even your deaf and dumb and
dead of limb are shaking with dread.

CUAUHTEMOC
Any human would. Monstrous creatures
have been spotted in our streets. They're
said to be Thistlemen, with two heads and
just one body.

MAGICIAN
Thistlemen. O my lord, if this is true, then –

MOTECUHZOMA

Hear me now: I dreamt that my dead sister
returned from the shadow world. She was
very distraught – she had seen strange, light-
skinned men there. And I dreamt about the
old fisherman bringing me his sea bird, the
netted crane, whose head was a mirror of
obsidian. I looked into this mirror and saw
weird creatures, winged denizens of the
crag, not of this world. This strange host of
people was charging at me across a plain.
They were armed for battle.

MAGICIAN

A great mystery shall come to pass. And it
shall come quickly.

MOTECUHZOMA

Tell me what all of this means.

MAGICIAN

Your seers and magicians shall look into
the water jugs; we'll tie the knots and untie
them again. And we'll look deep into the
blackest mirrors, my Lor –

MOTECUHZOMA

– Smash the mirrors! No one shall see what
I have seen. No one shall dream what I have
dreamt. *No one shall see the fall of the City
of Mexico.* Find the dreamers – find them
and shackle them, and turn them over to the
Keeper of the House of Darkness.

A painful radiance fills the screen, as it would be for eyes
gazing at the sun.

MOTECUHZOMA (*O.S.*)
Blind them. No one shall ever dream my
dream –

The sound of the rushing sea fades in. The brightness on the screen becomes white forms: waves crashing forth, seawater foaming, a beach. Now something slowly grows above the sea, spreading like gossamer, then billowing like soft cotton. Clouds? An apparition? Is the blinding light playing tricks on us?

At last we see what must be white sails bulging in the distance, the sails of dreams, like a floating vision. We can barely make out the hulls of the ships: there may be several galleons, all lined up like one long, floating, boggling body.

DISSOLVE TO

EXTERIOR. BEACH. DAY.

A simple, tattered fisherman, petrified with fear, stands on the beach straining to look out to sea, as lapping waves wash away his dugout canoe's fresh trail in the sand.

CLOSE-UP: A HORRIFIED ASTONISHMENT EN-LARGES HIS FACE.

The fisherman bolts. In a wild panic he flings his paddle and flees inland. The waves keep pounding the beach, un-disturbed, unresponding, without compassion. As always, Creation leers at the trials of man with contemptuous in-difference.

MAIN TITLES APPEAR.

DISSOLVE TO

EXTERIOR. TROPICAL JUNGLE. DAY.

A quick montage of landscapes. The fisherman hurtles down a muddy path beneath sagging branches, ferns and fronds.

FAST DISSOLVE TO

EXTERIOR. MOUNTAIN PLATEAU. DAY.

A lofty, barren plateau. Dust. Cacti. Towering peaks beyond. The fisherman, out of danger and no longer needing to flee, now races instead toward a precise destination with dire purpose. Four warriors accompany him.

FAST DISSOLVE TO

EXTERIOR. MOUNTAIN PASS. DAY.

Icy wind, hail. A steep slope disappears behind rushing clouds as the exhausted fisherman is helped through this perilous pass by an escort of ten warriors and runners, randomly collected en route, who have wrapped him in a heavy blanket to keep him warm. Feverishly pushing through the rocky notch, they steam like horses, gasping and panting in frozen gusts.

FAST DISSOLVE TO

EXTERIOR. LAKE OF MEXICO. DAY.

Countless canoes smoothly move about the vast pool of azure. A busy causeway leads to the island upon which the City of Mexico, Tenochtitlan, is set. The silhouetted imperial center looms above its bed of mist like a mirage. Temples, towers, palaces, canals. Just as we want to see more, the vista fades.

INTERIOR. MOTECUHZOMA'S PALACE. DUSK.

A spacious hall in the palace. Motecuhzoma sits on a mat playing a board game, vaguely reminiscent of backgammon, with exquisitely shaped jade stones. His opponent is wizened King Nezahualpilli. Servants attend. There is a tumbling, juggling dwarf.

Voices and commotion, then an agitated crowd pushes in. The Keeper of the House of Darkness walks to Motecuhzoma and whispers something in his ear. A curt nod is the sovereign's response.

The fisherman is hauled in. Courtiers, scribes, servants and guards swarm in after him, immediately averting their eyes from Motecuhzoma as they press against the wall and peer down at the floor.

The fisherman crawls more than walks, with his feet, knuckles and knees raw and bruised. He kisses the ground and remains lying at Motecuhzoma's feet.

MOTECUHZOMA
Who are you? Where do you come from?

FISHERMAN
O god and lord, forgive me – I'm just a
common man, from a village near
Cempoala.

MOTECUHZOMA
And what do you have to report?

FISHERMAN
I – I saw a mountain range floating on the
sea, very far away. The peaks were white,
white with snow. Wood... (*he struggles*)
Wooden...

> MOTECUHZOMA
> Speak.

> FISHERMAN
> Wooden mountains are approaching our
> coast. My lord, we have never seen anything
> like this.

Motecuhzoma turns to the Keeper of the House of Darkness.

> MOTECUHZOMA
> Throw him into the House of Darkness.
> Guard him well. Send scouts and our finest
> artist to the coast – have him make sketches
> for me.

EXTERIOR. COAST. DAWN.

CLOSE-UP: A HAND SKETCHES A SPANISH
GALLEON ON ROUGH PAPER.

The simple sketch, almost childlike, is skillfully rendered by
a hastening hand: a Spaniard fishing in a dinghy is drawn
with extraordinary speed, followed by a tree with an Aztec
spying from its branches.

The sound of the rushing sea as Spanish voices approach,
the conversation punctuated by a hearty laugh.

P.O.V. ARTIST: THROUGH LEAVES, TIP OF MAST,
FLUTTERING FLAG, BIT OF FURLED MAINSAIL
VIEWED FROM AFAR.

The artist hidden in the tree's thick foliage sketches urgent-
ly. Two Aztec scouts hiding close by strain to see the shore.
Abruptly they freeze and hold their breath as two of the
Spanish voices wander alarmingly near.

P.O.V. SCOUTS, THROUGH BRANCHES: TWO
SPANISH MEN PASS BELOW.

Their catch of fish slung over their shoulders, the two strange
men pause to share another hearty laugh, oblivious to the spies
overhead, then wander on.

INTERIOR. MOTECUHZOMA'S PALACE. TWILIGHT.

A guard lights torches around the room as Motecuhzoma,
transfixed by the sketches in his hands, stands over the bowed
artist, back from the coast.

                    MOTECUHZOMA
          And so it is true.

                    ARTIST
          They were fishing from a small boat, some
          with poles and others with nets. They
          stayed until late, then went back to their
          wood towers and climbed up into them.

                    MOTECUHZOMA
          Apparently they're not naked. What's that
          around their loins?

                    ARTIST
          Their legs were wrapped in long hose. Some
          wore blue jackets, others wore red or black
          or green. A few wore large round hats to
          shade their faces, for they have very light
          skin, much lighter than ours. And they have
          odd tufts of hair on their chins.

Motecuhzoma is crestfallen, staring downward a while without saying a word.

EXTERIOR. GREAT PYRAMID, TENOCHTITLAN. DAY.

A colossal cut-stone pyramid is the center of the Aztec capital, with two chapels on the top terrace housing Mexico's two holiest godheads. The steep steps of the Great Temple are stained with blood from human sacrifices.

Motecuhzoma ascends the pyramid. Hooded, black-cloaked priests try to assist him, but indignantly the sovereign shakes them off. As the camera floats upward beside him, widening the perspective of the city, the miracle of this mighty metropolis seems but a placid mirage set against the suppressed fury of the emperor.

Built on a flat island surrounded by a large lake, Tenochtitlan is connected to the mainland by several spoked causeways. Canoes skim about the lake and along the network of canals coursing through the city. We see gardens on the edge of town, a belt of reeds in the shallows and, then, in perfect geometric order, gardens floating in the distance. On the faraway mainland, we can make out numerous towns and villages, with the snow-capped silhouettes of two great volcanoes in the crystalline air beyond.

The emperor has reached the pyramid's topmost terrace. The priests of the sacred shrine welcome him deferentially, supporting him by his arms, but he spurns their help with a brusque gesture.

It takes him a few seconds to catch his breath. Becalmed now, his voice assumes a firm, dangerous tone.

MOTECUHZOMA
Am I to understand that you waver?

Silence. Their long hair tangled and matted with dry blood, the priests trade glances.

The two high priests take charge and step forward, hesitantly.

PRIEST 1
But this is the most precious, the most
sacred treasure we have. And –

PRIEST 2
– And it is not our property. It belongs to
our god. To Quetzalcoatl. Himself.

MOTECUHZOMA
That is correct. Our god has returned.

The shocked priests stand there, terrified by the stark enormity of the task at hand

MOTECUHZOMA
Hear this word, take this word: bring me
His holy vestments. Bring His cloak of
Quetzal feathers, His sandals and turquoise
mask. Bring the feathered breastplate, the
divining rod, the god's entire regalia – and
bring them now. You do understand: I said
now –

The priests silently fetch the god's vestments from the chapel's dark interior, and spread them reverently before their ruler.

MOTECUHZOMA
Our god has returned. He has descended
from the clouds above the Eastern Sea to
reclaim His throne. Before He vanished on
His raft of snakes, He promised to return
for the end of the world, and our faith in
His word has been justified. So, then, now –
what am *I*? Am I not the humble custodian
of His throne? Is that not so?

PRIEST 1
Yes, my lord, or – maybe we should –

PRIEST 2
– in fact, strictly speaking, if, perhaps, it isn't –

Motecuhzoma's wrathful glance instantly silences them.

MOTECUHZOMA
From now on, I trust no one but the gods.

EXTERIOR. COURTYARD OF PALACE. DAY.

An inner courtyard in the palace, magnificently overgrown
with flowers and vines. Cages with exotic birds of lavish
plumage abound, their cries echoing through the shady
arcades, fountains and trickling water everywhere. A docile
ocelot playfully paws a rubber ball.

Motecuhzoma, clearly quite agitated and driven, saunters
aimlessly across the courtyard, followed by Cuitlahuac. As
he walks he sniffs an orchid in his hand, tossing his words
over his shoulder to his older brother.

MOTECUHZOMA
The sages have reviewed the archives. The
men from the sea are no aliens. They are
gods. Our gods, returning to their homeland.

CUITLAHUAC
But, now, have we not made this land grow
and prosper in their absence? Aren't their
children, the Aztecs, masters of the world?
Mighty and rightfully proud? What about
them?

MOTECUZOMA
We have endreamed a kingdom worthy of
our gods. As my older brother, you have

12

been bypassed in the royal succession
because –

CUITLAHUAC

Dear brother, have I ever questioned the
ruling of our Crown Council?

MOTECUHZOMA

You were bypassed because there is a far
greater mission for you: *you* will be the one
to greet the gods. I order you to go to the
coast at once. Get there as fast as possible –
never stop, linger nowhere. Go to the floating towers, and dress the Most Holy One
– our lord God, Himself – in His vestments.

CUITLAHUAC

I – I am –

MOTECUHZOMA

Speak.

CUITLAHUAC

I am not afraid. But no one, neither you nor
I, is prepared for this.

MOTECUHZOMA

Take heart. There's but one thing for you to
do: you shall pay reverence to the god on
my behalf. Go and meet Him. Go and hear
Him. Listen and remember. Say that His
servant Motecuhzoma sent you. Give Him
His food and drink, as well as ours. You'll
know He's our god by which food He
reaches for first.

CUITLAHUAC

I'll summon my peers and porters. We'll
leave at once.

EXTERIOR. COAST. DAY.

The same sandy bay from which the fisherman had fled. Empty, no ships, nothing. A group of porters with head-bands holding burdens on their backs, and a few Aztec nobles, led by Cuitlahuac. Several naked children stand around something that has floated ashore, a bit of it rising out of the sand. No one dares to dig out the peculiar curio.

MEDIUM CLOSE-UP: HALF-CRUSHED SPANISH CHEST FILLED WITH SAND.

Cuitlahuac eyes each of the children inquisitively. A fearless little girl approaches Cuitlahuac and points beyond the far rim of the bay.

GIRL
There, over there – that's where they went.

EXTERIOR. OPEN SEA. DAWN.

The sea seems to be holding its breath, the water smooth as glass, unstirring.

Fog mists above the surface. Not a sound.

A large dugout glides away from the shore in reticence, its oarsmen scarcely daring to dip their paddles in the water. On board are Cuitlahuac and three Aztec noblemen, all of whom are wearing elegantly embroidered cloaks. They stare forward fixedly.

P.O.V. ENVOYS: SPANISH GALLEONS, MOTIONLESS IN THE MIST.

There they are, half real, because only the silence is real.

EXTERIOR. SPANISH FLAGSHIP. EARLY MORNING.

The dugout drifts to a halt alongside the weathered Spanish flagship. The anxious envoys look up toward the deck.

P.O.V. BOATMEN: CROWDING SPANISH FACES STARING DOWN AT THEM.

Some Spaniards are helmeted, and aim loaded muskets right at us. A man's voice bellows down to the envoys, too loud for such a short distance. In his incomprehensible Spanish he barks a question, then curses. Then a female voice.

> MALINCHE (O.S.)
> Identify yourselves! Who are you?

All eyes fall upon the speaker, Malinche, her resolute eyes bright with intelligence. She is copper-skinned and unusually pale, with a splendid figure and fine features.

> CUITLAHUAC
> But who are *you*? Aren't you one of us?

> MALINCHE
> I *was* one of you – but *I'm* the one asking
> questions here. What are you here for?
> Where are you from?

> CUITLAHUAC
> We have journeyed far, all the way from the
> City of Mexico, Tenochtitlan. Our ruler
> Motecuhzoma sent us.

> MALINCHE
> Then come aboard. All of you.

Amid the muzzles of muskets, a ladder lowers and helping hands reach down.

EXTERIOR. ON DECK. MORNING.

The deck of a capacious galleon. Masts, rigging, groaning ropes, barrels and balls of sailcloth, and a ladder dangling to a dinghy. In the apprehensive hush, gathered Spaniards form a theatrical tableau.

CLOSE-UP: WILD, RAPACIOUS SEAMEN WITH DEVIOUS, RAVENOUS EYES.

A handsome folding seat with inlaid mother-of-pearl, set on a raised platform under a red satin canopy. Richly clad like some grandiose aristocrat, his stylish hat sporting a huge ostrich plume, elegant Hernán Cortés sits in regal pose.

CLOSE-UP, FACE OF CORTÉS: CURIOUS EYES LURKING VEHEMENCE.

Cortés is flanked by his standard bearer and a rugged cannon. Next to the cannon stands wickedly handsome Pedro de Alvarado, as handsome as a blonde Nordic god. Just behind Cortés, Malinche takes position as Cuitiahuac and his entourage step aboard.

CLOSE-UP: CORTÉS' MANICURED HAND TENDERLY TAKES MALINCHE'S.

> MALINCHE (*Spanish*)
> I'll conduct the conversation, and translate
> it for you later. I know how to handle them.

Cortés nods in agreement as the Aztecs lay tamales, fruit and tortillas on mats, followed by the complete array of the ornate sacred vestments. Among the curious Spanish onlookers we discern two conspicuous figures: Father Olmedo in his priestly attire, alongside Gerónimo de Aguilar, squatting in the manner of the coastal Indians and wearing nothing but a loincloth on his tattooed body.

As an Aztec envoy burns copal in an earthenware basin, fanning the smoke into Cortés' face, another one slices his own ear ceremoniously, with several deep cuts.

CLOSE-UP: THE ENVOY'S BLOOD COLLECTS INSIDE A GOLDEN CUP.

Cuitlahuac sprinkles the blood on the arrayed foodstuffs. He kisses the deck at Cortés' feet and offers him the food. Cortés turns away in disgust, Alvarado gags and spits furiously. Malinche flips the blood overboard with a cold, casual toss, holding on to the cup.

Briefly Cortés whispers to her. She turns to the emissaries and points to the gold cup.

> MALINCHE
> My lord wishes to know if this cup is made
> of gold.

> CUITLAHUAC
> Yes, it is. Of course it's gold.

> MALINCHE
> The gentleman wants to have it.

Incredulous, Cuitlahuac makes no sense of this.

> MALINCHE
> He wants it.

> CUITLAHUAC
> But why? We have brought far more
> precious things for him. This cup is mere
> gold. It's worthless.

> MALINCHE
> Not in the hands of my master.

The golden cup is handed over. Cortés holds the repulsive thing with his fingertips while inspecting it, then sets it on the deck.

                    CUITLAHUAC
          Our ruler, Motecuhzoma, has commanded
          us to dress the white god in his vestments.
          We have preserved and protected the holiest
          and most precious of our treasures for him:
          the sacred feathers of the Quetzal bird.

                    MALINCHE
          So dress him.

The uncomprehending Spaniards ogle the golden cup as Malinche turns to Cortés, and changes languages.

                    MALINCHE (*Spanish*)
          They are going to dress you in some special
          clothes. It's quite important to them. Do it –
          I'll explain later.

Malinche turns back to Cuitlahuac.

                    MALINCHE
          Do it now.

                    CUITLAHUAC
          We do not follow the orders of an Aztec
          woman, or *any* human. We follow the
          orders of a god.

                    MALINCHE
          I'm the one you'll listen to; I'm the one they
          speak through. *I'm* the voice of the gods.

The envoys go to work, dressing Cortés with profound reverence in the god's regalia: sandals, breastplate, feathered cloak, studded turquoise mask. Upon removing Cortés' boots, the attending emissary reels from his reeking feet and fumigates them instantly with incense.

When they attach the mask, Cortés has had enough. He slams it on the deck, then throws off the feathered cloak and rips the gold plate from his chest, yanking out its feathers and flicking them into the wind. The horrified envoys slap their mouths repeatedly. Cortés springs to his feet and displays the golden disk, denuded like a plucked hen.

>CORTÉS (*Spanish*)
>And is this all? Is this is your gift of
>welcome? Is this how you greet people?

As Malinche quietly translates, Cortés subtly nods to Alvarado, who takes his cue.

CLOSE-UP: ALVARADO'S HAND LIGHTS THE CANNON'S SHORT FUSE.

A formidable blast into the hillside. Once the colossal cloud of smoke dissipates, we see the terrified envoys sprawled on the deck, with one slumped over the railing.

When given a signal from Cortés, the Spaniards clamp the fainted Aztecs in leg irons. Then the limp bundles of humanity are lifted and seated upright, only to sag back against the mainmast.

Cortés calls for a prepared package. He pulls the satin wrapping off to reveal a chain of green glass beads, a couple of biscuits from the ship's pantry and a brocaded Flemish cap.

Cortés approaches Cuitlahuac and forces the gift into his limp, unresponding hands. Malinche leans over the emissaries with sisterly concern.

MALINCHE
My lord gives you this with all his heart for
your lord, Motecuhzoma. And when he gets
it, you must tell him that my lord would
like to visit him. He himself is but an envoy
of a mighty emperor, who rules the world.

Cuitlahuac's eyes focus on a helmet of one of the Spanish
soldiers close by.

CUITLAHUAC
I would like to thank you for these noble
gifts for my lord. But – if it would be
possible to take one of your metal head-
dresses to him, that my lord Motecuhzoma
might behold it himself, I would be most
grateful.

CORTÉS/MALINCHE
You may have it. But it must be returned to
me, filled with gold dust.

EXTERIOR. NEAR THE SPANISH FLAGSHIP.

The Aztec emissaries have been unshackled and already sit
in their dugout, paddles in hand. Cuitlahuac is the last to
descend the ladder into the canoe, with Spanish hands
assisting him. Then the hooked pole joining the small craft
with the galleon is lifted.

At once the oarsmen start rowing maniacally, their peers
paddling with bare hands like men possessed, and the canoe
shoots straight towards shore.

EXTERIOR. PALACE ENTRANCE. NIGHT.

Commotion at the torchlit gate. The exhausted envoys have
returned but the rigid Royal Guards will not admit them,
grimly barring their way with spears.

CUITLAHUAC

But you *must*! Even if he's sleeping! Tell
him that the ones he sent to the middle of
the water have returned.

The lead guard vacillates. An envoy urgently speaks up.

ENVOY

We have seen something absolutely
horrifying, something no one's ever seen
before!

The lead guard now realizes the situation's gravity. Quickly
he disappears into the palace to wake Motecuhzoma.

INTERIOR. ANTEROOM TO MOTECUHZOMA'S
BEDCHAMBER. NIGHT.

A small cubicle, dark but for the torchlight flickering against
the intense faces of Cuitlahuac and Motecuhzoma, who has
just been roused from sleep. They inspect the Spanish infantryman's helmet.

CUITLAHUAC

They seemed to be men, but I'm not so sure.
Which is why I knew I must show you this.

MOTECUHZOMA

So this does it. Our scientists and priests
have never produced an explanation for this
strange thing, this headdress worn by our
god.

CUITLAHUAC

We have seen it every day when we have
bowed before Him in His temples, and
pondered its mystery. But maybe now, at
last, the secret of its sacred nature is
revealed.

MOTECUHZOMA

For me this is the final proof. Those
creatures from beyond the sea are our gods,
returned at last.

INTERIOR. GREAT THRONE ROOM. MIDNIGHT.

Motecuhzoma on his throne, with the Crown Council on
mats before him. The chamber is jammed with high-ranking
officials, warriors, priests, magicians and dwarfs. Everyone
strains to subdue their excitement, their curiosity and fear.

Cortés' gifts have been spread before Motecuhzoma, who
examines the glass beads in wonder.

MOTECUHZOMA

You have been to a very dangerous place.
You have looked the gods in the face, and
the gods have truly spoken to you.

ENVOY 1

It isn't a language. They just scream these
very rough noises.

ENVOY 2

Some of them were dressed head to toe in
metal, covering every part of their bodies.
They only bared their faces, which were like
chalk, and some of them…

ENVOY 1

And some of them had yellow hair. Like the
rays of the sun.

CUITLAHUAC

My lord, I saw the Sun God Himself.

ENVOY 2

One of the men was *black*; he actually wore
black skin. He moved with the Sun, and was
always right behind him, like a shadow. His
purpose wasn't clear to us.

CUITLAHUAC

We suspect he was the Sun's eclipse.

MOTECUHZOMA

And the lightning from their metal rods?

ENVOY 1

A shower of fire came bursting out, and a
clap of thunder. And when the round pellet
spat forth and struck a hill by the beach, it
was as if the hill fell apart, and crumbled.
And when it struck a tree, the tree splintered, and seemed to vanish.

ENVOY 2

The smoke smelled very foul; it had a putrid
odor that wounded my head.

ENVOY 1

And the strangers themselves – you know,
my lord, those gods really *stink*. They never
wash as we Aztecs do.

A pause. Motecuhzoma meditates, and something starts
working inside him. Then he speaks, his voice very low, all
emotion subdued.

MOTECUHZOMA

What will happen to us now? Who is truly
in command? Alas, until now, I. My heart is
in utter torment. It burns. It truly hurts. Yet
nothing can be done. All my dreams have
spoken.

Stillness. Long seconds pass before someone in the Crown Council stirs. It is old Nezahualpilli, who dares to speak.

> NEZAHUALPILLI
> But how can they be gods if they want no blood? If they refuse the most precious offering men can make?

> CUAUHTEMOC
> And – please forgive me for saying this – how can they be gods if *this* is what they eat?

He points to the ship's rusk biscuits. Motecuzoma wavers momentarily, relieved that there is someone present who doesn't share his dark mood. He contemplates the biscuit, then takes a cautious nibble from it and passes it on to a dwarf, who more courageously takes a bite. All eyes are upon him as the dwarf chews with loud crunches.

CLOSE-UP: THE DWARF BOLDLY CHEWS ON THE BISCUIT.

Prompted by Motecuhzoma's signal, old Nezahualpilli also tastes it.

> NEZAHUALPILLI
> It tastes like pumice stone.

> CUAUHTEMOC
> And what's more, besides that, would a real god ever rip up his sacred cloak?

A furious glance from Motecuhzoma. Everyone visibly holds their breath. But Nezahualpilli keeps munching and crunching noisily, albeit more slowly.

CLOSE-UP: NEZAHUALPILLI CHEWS LOUDLY, SLOWLY.

CLOSE-UP: STERN MOTECUHZOMA PONDERS.

> MOTECUHZOMA
> Hear this word, take this word. This is my
> command. Guard the entire coast, watch
> what those alien creatures do. From now on
> we must study their every move. Cuauhte-
> moc, find out who the Aztec woman is who
> speaks for those... gods.

EXTERIOR. COAST. DAY.

CLOSE-UP: A HAND DEFTLY SKETCHES SPANISH
DISEMBARKMENT SCENE.

A simple but precise drawing in the style of the Aztecs:
several galleons moored in a bay, sand dunes, cargo strewn
everywhere, horses, a cow, two sheep and a creature that
bears some resemblance to a boar. A few Spaniards wear
armor, their shirtless peers push cargo chests down a barge's
plank.

CLOSE-UP: FINISHED SKETCH IS FLIPPED OVER
AND A NEW ONE BEGUN.

The prow of a barge is drawn, a plank, then a Spaniard dragging a reluctant horse ashore.

FAST DISSOLVE TO

EXTERIOR. COAST. DAY.

The actual Spaniard drags the actual reluctant horse down
the plank, with others behind it dragged off the barge as
well, bucking and shying. Spaniards yell and curse, a horse
plunges into the water. Coastal Indians enlisted by the
Spaniards drop their loads and flee.

The entire Spanish force has but sixteen horses. Now gathered on shore, frightened, seasick and unsure of their footing, they sway and stagger about.

EXTERIOR. SPANISH COASTAL SETTLEMENT. LATE AFTERNOON.

Amid the chaos of this crude settlement, a cross between a military encampment and a construction site, a petrified Indian porter, bent over with a load of wood on his back, trembles as a huge Spanish mastiff hound sniffs him. The second the poor fellow tries to move; the dog growls and snaps at him.

Several ragged porters bearing firewood approach. They quickly set their burdens by the makeshift clay oven and help the last porter remove his strapped load with unusual deference. When two Spaniards come and haul off the mean hound, this last porter furtively turns away, locking eyes with a porter who dives down and kisses the sand at the young man's feet.

CLOSE-UP: THE YOUNG MAN IN PORTER'S GUISE IS CUAUHTEMOC.

Motecuhzoma's nephew mutters to the bowed porter with subdued fury.

> CUAUHTEMOC (*low*)
> Stand up, you fool.

The porter scrambles to his feet.

> PORTER
> My lord, I –

> CUAUHTEMOC (*low*)
> Don't call me "lord"! Now, what did you
> observe at their hideout?

He inconspicuously cocks his head toward an enclosure of four hanging mats, from which a Spaniard emerges, buttoning his trousers. It seems to be a latrine.

> PORTER (*low*)
> My Lo –

Cuauhtemoc's glance makes the man choke on his words.

> CUAUHTEMOC (*low*)
> Tell me why they hide in there!

> PORTER (*low*)
> They – they drain themselves in there. They relieve themselves, like humans do.

Suddenly Cuauhtemoc spots something and pulls the porter into a thicket.

> CUAUHTEMOC (*low*)
> *Sshhh! Get down –*

From the woodland shadows they watch a young Spanish soldier return with his water-filled helmet to a tiny plot of ground he has weeded. He stabs his sword into the soil to make some holes. Then he withdraws something from his pocket.

CLOSE-UP: HIS BOYISH FACE GLOWS AS HE OGLES A HANDFUL OF SEEDS.

He crouches and plants the seeds in the holes. After covering them with earth, he sprinkles them with water from his helmet, as voices suddenly call from the settlement.

> VOICES (*O.S.*)
> Bernal! Bernal Díaz! Where the hell are you!

Bright, young Bernal Díaz pricks up his ears, then hurries off. Once he's gone, Cuauhtemoc and the porter leave the thicket and dig up the planted seeds.

CLOSE-UP: TWO SHINY ORANGE SEEDS IN CAUHTEMOC'S HAND.

The Aztecs have never seen orange pits before. They turn them over and hold them up to the light. A nearby rustling of leaves, footsteps and hushed chatter. Cuauhtemoc quickly steals away with his discovery.

EXTERIOR. PALACE COURTYARD ARCADE. MORNING.

The lush tropical courtyard: water trickles in languid pools, a parrot talks to himself, the sunbathing ocelot yawns by a fountain. Motecuhzoma stands with Cuauhteroc by a flower bed where two small holes have been dug, wondrously contemplating something in his hand.

CLOSE-UP: BERNAL'S TWO PITS IN MOTECUHZO-MA'S HAND.

Full of admiration, the ruler stares at the unfamiliar seeds. One of them has already begun to sprout.

> MOTECUHZOMA
> Do you think a flower will grow from this?
> Or some kind of vine?

Cuauhtemoc has other things on his mind.

> CUAUHTEMOC
> Oh, I would say it's either fruit, or poison.
> But the most significant thing I discovered
> is that the aliens have been fighting among
> themselves. They even hung one of their
> own from a tree. Yet they –

Motecuhzoma is too entranced by the seeds to listen.

MOTECUHZOMA

Maybe they're a new grain, something we
have never known, or a different type of
tobacco –

CUAUHTEMOC

– yet some of the coastal tribes are
intimidated by them, and have already
taken their side.

This gets Motecuhzoma's attention, but just partly. And
when Cuitlahuac joins them as Cuauhtemoc continues, the
ruler hardly acknowledges his brother.

CUAUHTEMOC

You know, they ride really miraculous stags
of some sort. I saw them – they're enormous. They stomp like thunder, as if the
stars were raining down from the sky, and
leave scars where their hooves touch the
ground. But I know we can kill them.

Motecuhzoma kneels to put the two orange pits in the holes.
At once his gardener covers the seeds with earth, while a
priest waves smoking incense over them.

CUITLAHUAC

Their force is small. Surely we outnumber
them.

CUAUHTEMOC

Of course we do. We have counted them,
and there are about four hundred. It would
take us no time at all to send sixty thousand
warriors to fight them. And if we did, it
would take but a few hours to destroy them.

EXTERIOR. COAST. DAY.

Lovely Malinche wanders dreamlost along the strand, away from the makeshift settlement, singing to herself.

> MALINCHE
> *Little flower, little flower, I am flowering,*
> *too –*

MED. CLOSE-UP: MALINCHE STIRS FROM REVERIE, SENSING SOMETHING.

Now humming instead, she pauses, then turns and heads into the woods. Suddenly she pivots and lunges for something behind a tree, where she clutches an Indian noblewoman's arm. Malinche and the older woman are face to face.

> MALINCHE
> What are you doing, spying like a weasel
> in the bush? What will you report to your
> leaders? Why are you spying on these men?

> NOBLEWOMAN
> I'm not. I'm spying on *you.*

> MALINCHE
> Why? What for?

> NOBLEWOMAN
> I was "spying" on you because I have never
> seen a more beautiful woman, anywhere.

Malinche studies the woman's eyes, her grip firm.

> MALINCHE
> And?

> NOBLEWOMAN
> And I want to save your life.

Slowly Malinche looses her grip on the matron's arm.

MALINCHE
What do you mean by that? Who are you?

NOBLEWOMAN
I am the wife of a Cempoalan nobleman
who is our ruler's chief counsel. Because of
this, I know all that goes on at the highest
levels of government. And right now there's
a lot going on, with much more to come. It
will be brutal. But if you listen to me and
agree to what I propose, and *only* if you
do, then your life will be spared from the
bloodshed to come.

MALINCHE
Tell me. I will listen.

The wary noblewoman guides Malinche by the elbow away
from the woods, almost whispering as they walk.

MALINCHE
So why will there be bloodshed?

NOBLEWOMAN
Because no one shall *ever* degrade our gods.
The moment they reach Cempoala, they shall
be captured. As you will be, unless you act
wisely, and remain true to yourself and your
people.

Malinche listens closely, feigning interest.

MALINCHE
I shall never betray my people. What is it you
want me to do?

NOBLEWOMAN
I have a handsome son of noble blood. It
is my sincere wish that he find a woman to
marry, someone of strength and intelligence
and beauty, to match his stature. Someone
like you.

Malinche conceals her true feelings by leading the woman on.

MALINCHE
Can I believe this? That you'll free me from
this bondage? And take me away from those
slavemasters? When will it be – tonight?
May I leave with you now?

NOBLEWOMAN
No, not yet. But soon. First you must go
with them on the road to Cempoala, and –

EXTERIOR. SPANISH CAMP. EVENING.

Partly visible through the firelit maze of supplies, animals
and lean-tos are Cortés and Malinche, dining on a makeshift table by candlelight, in the middle of discreet, muted
conversation.

MALINCHE (*low*)
– and as soon as our entire force is within
the city gates, just when it seems that all of
Cempoala has come to welcome you, the
elite warriors, their ruler's royal guard, will
capture you, and everyone else. They have
actually prepared cages. I fear for you, my
lord.

CORTÉS (*low*)
No, mi corazon – no te preocupes. But these
cages –

> MALINCHE (*low*)
> The cages are meant to carry you and your
> men to the capital for sacrifice. They are
> ready and waiting.

Cortés tenderly places his hand on hers.

> CORTÉS
> If we show weakness now, we'll be cut to
> pieces. Believe me – even the stones will rise
> against us.

EXTERIOR. PYRAMID OF CEMPOALA. NIGHTFALL.

The distant horizon has a deathly glow from the fires con-
suming Cempoala. On the pyramid's lofty terrace, Cortés,
Malinche, Alvarado and several Spanish soldiers with drawn
swords have gathered. Before Cortés, six Indian dignitaries,
priests and nobles, prostrate themselves on the ground.

> DIGNITARIES
> We have been destroyed! We're nothing!
> Completely annihilated!

Indignant Cortés shouts at them in Spanish and Malinche
translates.

> CORTÉS (*Spanish*)
> Stand up!

> PRIEST
> We bow before a god.

> CORTÉS (*Spanish*)
> I'm no god.

> PRIEST
> Only a god can defeat thousands and
> thousands of Aztecs with just a handful of
> men.

NOBLE
We're no match for your lightning and
thunder. We can't stand up to your
miraculous stags. We can't stand up to –

He watches in horror as a group of Spaniards headed by
Alvarado topple an idol from its pedestal, then roll it across the
terrace and over the edge.

As Father Olmedo holds up a cross, Cortés delivers a speech,
which Malinche translates simultaneously.

CORTÉS/MALINCHE
We have freed you from your devils and
demons. From this moment on, the True
Cross is planted here, and there shall be no
more human sacrifice. For human sacrifice
is the work of *Satan*. And, if anyone should
attack us, this country's rightful lords, we
shall respond to them with all our might in
justified self-defense.

The priests weep and slap their mouths in their customary
expression of horror. Cortés brandishes his drawn sword
in a grandiose manner, then with three blows shatters a clay
urn smoking with copal incense. With sword upraised he
turns to the Spaniards, then the Indians, and proclaims:

CORTÉS/MALINCHE
I claim this land in the name of our
Emperor Charles! If anyone objects, I shall
defend the emperor's cause with my sword!

Father Olmedo begins to sing the *Te Deum*. Rising from the
darkening land is the chant of priests and soldiers.

EXTERIOR. SHORE. DAY.

What we notice first is disquieting: the Spanish ships seem to have been destroyed on purpose. There are beached, skeletal wrecks beaten by waves, charred planks tossing in the surf, splintered masts with limp rigging rising from the water.

Anything even vaguely usable has been stacked on shore: balls of sailcloth, iron parts, hawsers, planks. Most of it has been removed, with a few Spaniards hauling off what's left to their makeshift settlement beyond the dunes.

Cortés sits on the edge of the beach beneath his canopy, receiving an Aztec delegation led by Cuitlahuac. Besides him is a snorting, nervously prancing steed firmly reined by Alvarado. When the horse whinnies, it nearly scares the Aztecs to death.

Cuitlahuac composes himself and presents the borrowed Spanish helmet, now filled with gold dust, to Cortés. Then he hangs a heavy gold chain around Cortés' neck as a welcoming gift.

> CUITLAHUAC
> I welcome my lord with great joy, a joy that is
> tempered by sadness. My lord, Motecuhzoma,
> is ill. He begs your pardon for being unable to
> receive the returned gods personally. He
> wishes those who have descended from the
> clouds a happy voyage back across the sea.

He looks at the ruined ships and hesitates. A dark notion dawns on him.

> MALINCHE
> That's impossible. The ships no longer exist.
> My lord has burned his bridges. Now there
> is no turning back.

CORTÉS (*Spanish*)
I came here from across the sea. I will now
move on to your city of Tenochtitlan, to
deliver a message there from my emperor.

A flurry of confusion among the Aztec delegates. Cuitlahuac makes another attempt to dissuade Cortés from marching inland.

CUITLAHUAC
But the roads are poor. They're practically
impassable. As much as we would like to
help you on your way, our stock of provisions would be inadequate for your army.

Cortés and Malinche quickly confer. He seems quite calm and cryptic, while she takes on an angry, commanding tone.

MALINCHE
Aren't there quite enough provisions for
your army, the sixty thousand you sent
against us? Don't try to play games with us.
My lord shall move on to the City of
Mexico, whether Motecuhzoma likes it or
not.

Malinche realizes she may have gone too far with her tactics, that this might lead to a conflict that Cortés would never survive. She signals Cortés with an intimate glance; instantly he changes his demeanor and becomes effusively affable, quickly standing to give his Aztec guest an exquisite inlaid folding chair like his own, amiably demonstrating how to open and fold it.

Next Cortés shoves a painted image of the Madonna into Cuitlahuac's hands, and addresses him in a warm, friendly tone, as Malinche cordially translates.

CORTÉS/MALINCHE
This is for your lord Motecuhzoma. The
picture shows the Blessed Virgin with her
Most Precious Child. He's the Son of God.
You are to have your lord raise this image in
his temple right away, and pay it homage.

Cuitlahuac holds the icon without comprehension. Then
he signals a couple of porters, who set four bundles before
Cortés containing a small treasure of gold objects.

Instantly the Spaniards surge forward. Even Cortés can
barely control himself.

CUITLAHUAC
This is for the strangers, our friends. So they
may return home, happy and content.

The Spaniards can no longer hold themselves back. Fierce
pushing and shoving. Cuitlahuac is nearly knocked over.

INTERIOR. PALACE THRONE ROOM. DAY.

Motecuhzoma sits on his throne, deeply pensive. The
Crown Council is assembled. Cuitlahuac is standing before
it, presenting his report.

CUITLAHUAC
They wallowed in that gold like swine.
Their eyes glowed, they laughed, they
slapped each other's back. The truth is, they
hungered like pigs for that stuff.

NEZAHUALPILLI
We have blundered there. Now they'll want
more and more.

As the Council members look at one another, Motecuhzoma starts to call the old man to order for speaking out
of turn, but balks. Instead, the monarch's mien grows ever
darker. He says nothing. Cuitlahuac changes the subject.

> CUITLAHUAC
> As for the Aztec woman with the strangers,
> I found out that she's a slave, an orphan
> given to them by the ruler of Cempoala.
> But there's something about her past that
> she's hiding, I don't know what. Should we
> continue to investigate?

No answer from Motecuhzoma. Cuitlahuac persists, trying
yet another subject.

> CUITLAHUAC
> The strangers' lord embraced me, and said
> he came in peace. He asked if Motecuh-
> zoma is young or old. He asked, "What
> sort of man is he? A youth, perhaps?
> Or already old? Maybe he's advanced in
> years, already white-haired." To which I
> answered, "He's a mature man, his body
> strong but rather slender – spare, tall and
> thin." In my opinion, he asked me not out
> of friendship, but out of a need to know
> just what kind of warrior is leading us.

Ever more morose, Motecuhzoma tries to mask his growing
fear.

> MOTECUHZOMA
> Why was I brought here? Why was I born
> into this time, if only to know woe?

Cuauhtemoc dares to take the floor.

CUAUHTEMOC
How can he speak of peace when he kills
our people? How will he return to his
homeland if he's destroyed his own floating
towers?

CUITLAHUAC
My lord, what choice do we have? We
should attack them at once. But this time we
won't be thrown back in panic by a single
stag, no matter how big, no matter how fast
or ferocious it is. They are mortal – we have
killed one of them. In just a few days we
could summon over a hundred thousand
warriors to fight them. But no one pays me
any heed. I guess I'm too *young*.

But plenty of people in the group are heeding him; they
look at him approvingly. Then all eyes turn to the gloomy
monarch. For a long time, he ponders. An oppressive stillness fills the room. Then, with head lowered, Motecuhzoma
speaks, almost inaudibly.

MOTECUHZOMA
My friends, what more can we do? Is there a
mountain high enough for us to flee to? Or
a cave where I can hide? Flight is my desire,
departure is my wish.

CUITLAHUAC
My brother, all we can do is await them.

He rallies himself and sits erect.

MOTECUHZOMA
We must send out our magicians and sorcerers against them – they can drive the strangers away with a spell. Or they can chant at
them to make them ill, or even kill them.

EXTERIOR. MOUNTAINS. DAY.

Rain is falling. Ragged clouds crawl up the slopes. The Spanish army struggles up a muddy path, wrapped in soaked woolen blankets, freezing, with their wounded carried in hammocks behind. The rear guard, wending its way with the others, consists of Indian warriors, auxiliary troops from near the coast.

Drenched Spaniards shoulder heavy muskets, one of them coughing and shaking with fever. Horsemen lead their steaming steeds by the reins. All weaponry and armor is covered with a fine rust.

Cortés dismounts, then tenderly lifts dripping Malinche onto his horse. It is clear that she's more than an instrument in the business of conquest as he walks on, reins in hand, chivalrously leading his lady.

The Indian auxiliary force, much larger than the Spanish, is unarmed, its warriors serving as porters. Forty Indians pull a heavy cannon up the slope with ropes. No conversation; sporadic calls and whistles echo off the mountain walls.

Two magicians wearing grand fans of feathers stand on a cliff.

P.O.V. MAGICIANS: THE SILENT ARMY BELOW PLODS UPHILL IN THE RAIN.

The magicians curse, and try to strike terror into the Spaniards and their allies with weird dramatic gestures. A massive Spanish combat dog takes note; when he charges at them, the feathered magicians flee.

EXTERIOR. LAKE OF MEXICO. SUNSET.

The sun sinks into the lake as canoes head homeward. The serene procession seems to bear something vague, something unspoken, something ominous.

EXTERIOR. PALACE ROOF. TWILIGHT.

His face aglow with the setting sun, Motecuhzoma sits atop his palace roof on the chair given to him by Cortés, gazing into the distance.

An extended Crown Council of twenty, including elite military officers, priests and scribes, sits on mats in front of him.

> MAGICIAN
> We're no match for them. We're no match
> for their *dogs*.

> CUAUHTEMOC
> They have enlisted our enemies, the people
> of Tlaxcala, to their cause, and they're
> provoking all the states that owe us tribute
> to revolt.

He hesitates. Now encouraging the young man, Motecuhzoma nods to him almost imperceptibly.

> CUAUHTEMOC
> And of course those who kept their faith in us,
> the people of Cempoala –

> NEZAHUALPILLI
> What people of Cempoala? Are there any
> left?

> CUAUHTEMOC
> Not very many. Those who managed to flee
> the bloodshed are hiding up in the mountains.
> The aliens came upon us like shadows from
> behind the stars. Yet, even so, we must still
> throw them back into the sea. And we will.

MOTECUHZOMA

We can't declare war on them – the season
for war isn't here yet. And even if it were,
first we must perform the proper rites, and
agree with them on the place to fight. But
can we *really* fight Quetzalcoatl, our returning lord, who is at once Time, and Night,
and Wind, as well as the planet Venus?

MAGICIAN

Venus *is* growing stronger.

MOTECUHZOMA

So, then: I order you to supply those
creatures with food from now on. That is
what they have demanded.

NEZAHUALPILLI

My advice is: no one should invite a man
into his house who might throw him out.

Motecuhzoma broods for a moment. He comes up with a
plan hatched from his most profound anxiety, as if he could
only delegate tasks which he himself can perform.

MOTECUHZOMA

Search for someone who looks like me, for
someone who bears a strong resemblance to
me. He and he alone can save us.

EXTERIOR. MOUNTAIN PASS. DAY.

A forbidding mountain pass, thirteen thousand feet above
sea level. The only thing growing here is a bit of thin grass
amid black volcanic sand. To one side rises the snow-capped
cone of Popocatepetl; on the other side, the equally tall
glacier atop Itzaciuatl glows brightly in the sunlight. From
Popocatepetl's peak comes a distant roar. The volcano spits white
smoke, which forms a cloud horizontal with the storm above.

The Spanish army and its Indian troops are bivouacked here, with campfires everywhere. Their smoke is violently blown away by the whipping winds.

Cortés seems to be ill. He's wrapped in blankets, with one of them pulled over his head, sipping a hot beverage.

CLOSE-UP: AILING CORTÉS' FEVERISH EYES AND SUNKEN CHEEKS.

Near Cortés are Malinche, Alvarado, a few Spanish leaders and a group of high-ranking Tlaxcalan dignitaries. Four Indian servants struggle to hang onto Cortés' canopy in the fierce whistling wind.

With his back to us, Motecuhzoma faces Cortés in his magnificent feathered raiment. He's accompanied by dignitaries, priests and servants. Cortés studies the Aztec ruler's face.

P.O.V. CORTÉS: THE MAN HAS FINE FEATURES AND A THIN BEARD, BUT HE IS *NOT* MOTECUH-ZOMA.

CORTÉS/MALINCHE
Are you the One? Are you Motecuhzoma?
Are you the Heart of Mexico?

MOTECUHZOMA'S DOUBLE
I am the humble custodian of your throne.
Yes, my lord – *I* am Motecuhzoma.

The Tlaxcalans urgently huddle and whisper to one another. Then a principal Tlaxcalan dignitary turns to the imposter and abruptly raises his voice.

DIGNITARY
Go! Get thee hence! Why do you lie to us?
What do you take us for? You cannot mock
us, you cannot infect our heads, you cannot

trick us, you cannot stare us down. We will
not look away. We will not turn our eyes
aside.

The dignitary glowers at him scornfully and continues.

DIGNITARY
You can't bewitch or bedazzle us – not you.
For Motecuhzoma is over there: he's there
in the City of Mexico! He'll be unable to
take refuge. Where will he go? Can he go
burrow into a mountainside and hide,
perchance? Is he a bird, perchance? Will he
take wing, perchance, and fly?

EXTERIOR. CITY OF MEXICO (TENOCHTITLAN).
DAY.

We move down a canal leading directly to the main market-
place. Empty. Nothing. The city is breathless. In the distance, a woman hustles into her house and shuts the door.

DISSOLVE TO

EXTERIOR. GRAND SQUARE. DAY.

The Grand Square in front of the temple. Empty. Nothing.
From far away we hear the steady, disquieting clang of a
gong. A turkey pops up, then disappears again.

DISSOLVE TO

EXTERIOR. CITY PERIPHERY. DAY.

The edge of town: no one in the gardens, abandoned boats,
no one out on the lake. The soft sound of the waves accen-
tuates the silence.

EXTERIOR. MOUNTAIN PASS. DAY.

Moving down the steep mountainside now. Wind rushing through the tall trees.

A path zigzags downward between the two volcanoes into the abyss. From an overlook the Spaniards get their first glimpse of the Lake of Mexico, the islands, the towns.

The Spanish army has come to a halt. Dumbfounded soldiers look down at the landscape below. They cannot believe their eyes.

CLOSE-UP: THE ASTONISHED BOYISH FACE OF BERNAL DIAZ.

> BERNAL (*Spanish*)
> Am I dreaming? Have we marched into
> some fairy tale?

EXTERIOR. PATH. DAY.

Further below. The well-trod path suddenly ends in dense maguey cacti. The Spanish army is forced to stop.

From above, descending soldiers push the men who have stopped. A heavy cannon separates the group coming down, dragging ten men behind it; the thing is simply too heavy for the Indian auxiliaries to manage. Finally the cannon comes to an abrupt halt by slamming into a massive tree trunk. Twigs and shards of bark shower down from the shaken tree.

Alvarado examines the cacti obstructing the way and sees that the path continues somewhat further down. He yanks out one of the prickly plants and kicks the next one with his boot.

> ALVARADO (*Spanish*)
> They have just been planted! Look at this!

The Spaniards start pulling out the plants and tossing them away. The procession resumes.

EXTERIOR. LAKE OF MEXICO. TWILIGHT.

Evening light. The lake lies still. A rim of reeds with a heron flying majestically above. The lake is empty; the only thing on its surface is a canoe elegantly festooned with gold-embroidered bunting, gliding quietly over the water. In the middle of the canoe, a regal canopy. Two oarsmen slowly push the boat forward with long poles.

Motecuhzoma sits beneath his canopy. He is pensive and melancholy. Outside the canopy, Nezahualpilli and Cuitlahuac sit facing each other. The boat glides almost soundlessly along. After a while, Motecuhzoma starts to speak. He weeps silent tears, but his soft voice remains firm.

> MOTECUHZOMA
> They're like locusts. They're like demons of
> the twilight, moving in ever smaller, closer
> circles –

He falls silent. The boat glides on. Then he gathers himself.

> MOTECUHZOMA
> O mighty lords, it is fitting that the three of
> us should be here to receive the gods, as I
> wish to find solace with you, and also bid you
> farewell. How little we enjoyed the realms
> bequeathed to us by our ancestors. Although
> they were powerful kings and lords, they left
> this world in peace and harmony. But sorrow
> is about to befall us. What have we done to
> deserve this fate? How did we offend our
> gods? Who are these beings who have come?
> There is only one remedy: we must make
> our hearts strong to endure what is about to
> happen. For they are at our gates.

He does not wait for any advice or reply. The canoe continues on its way. A red sunset lights the sky. A rushing flock of birds seeks its nesting place.

EXTERIOR. CAUSEWAY. MORNING.

The mile-long straight line of the causeway leading from the South into the City of Mexico. The Spaniards are advancing toward the city, and the entire population seems to crowd the causeway's margins. A colossal tension. Dead silence. Even the little children are totally silent. Thousands of canoes, brimming with curious onlookers, have maneuvered into position on both sides of the span.

The Spanish army approaches in precise formation. In front of the parade, huge combat dogs move to and fro, sniffing everything. The hushed crowds press back as far as the causeway allows. At the head of the formation, four riders side by side, letting their horses canter. They are dressed in noisy iron armor, their visors closed, their helmets plumed with ostrich feathers.

Behind them is the standard bearer, alone. He circles his flag in the air, making figure-eights. He exuberantly tosses the flag overhead and skillfully catches it. Trailing him are infantrymen with drawn swords, everyone in precisely ordered lines. After them come more horsemen, then marksmen with shouldered muskets, then crossbowmen. As they walk they keep loading their weapons with iron bolts, and aim at imaginary targets. Then a small gap, to accord greater significance to Cortés at the parade's end.

Cortés rides a beautiful chestnut stallion that canters nervously. He's accompanied by Malinche and several servants from his personal household. Among his coterie is the lone black man, Okello, who is dressed as a nobleman.

The Indian allies follow Cortés, again with some distance between him and their ranks. They have all painted their faces and armed themselves for war. The first of the Tlax-calans drag along the dull, thudding cannons on long ropes. The Indian troops chant rhythmical, low-pitched sounds which might be a battle song, although it has no melody.

Great suspense among the Spaniards. Just a small cluster of some four hundred men, they arrive in the capital city, in the midst of hundreds of thousands of enemies, on an island with accessways that can be easily cut off. Numerous breaks in the causeways are spanned by movable bridges, over which the horses' stomping hooves resound.

Cortés reins in his horse with regnant, high-handed gestures. He exudes the aura of the impassive, unflappable, unimpressed commander that he is.

EXTERIOR. ACACHINACO SQUARE. MORNING.

The causeway reaches the first houses of the city at Acachi-naco Square, which is bordered by whitewashed, flat-roofed dwellings. Crowds of curious Aztecs atop the houses look on in astonished silence.

Motecuhzoma emerges from the city interior with a large escort. He is carried by dignitaries on a sedan chair adorned with garlands of gold. Above the sedan chair is a canopy of gleaming green quetzal feathers, brocaded with woven braids of gold. The emperor, who wears a spectacular crown of feath-ers, nearly disappears beneath the flowers heaped upon him.

Kings from surrounding city-states owing tribute to the Aztecs sweep the path before him. Others spread their cloaks on the spot where the sedan chair is set down, so the emperor's feet won't touch the ground. Before the sedan chair, a dignitary carries a scepter adorned with gold and jade, representing the emperor's sovereignty.

The crowd on the square gives way. All eyes turn from their ruler. The people deferentially tap the ground with their fingers and kiss them. Everyone is barefoot, even the dignitaries and kings in the retinue.

Both processions have almost met, and now come to a halt. Cortés moves all the way to the front, where he dismounts and hands his horse's reins to Okello. At the same time, Motecuhzoma alights from his sedan chair. The two men stride toward each other.

Cortés tries to embrace the Aztec ruler, but Motecuhzoma's dignitaries block him from their untouchable sovereign. Motecuhzoma hangs a garland of flowers around Cortés' neck, then a magnificent gold chain. Now he's handed more garlands, which he hangs from the neck of Alvarado, who has opened his visor. Mistaking Okello for a nobleman, the emperor adorns him as well.

Cortés in kind carefully places a chain of glass beads around Motecuhzoma's neck. Everything has taken place in total silence; even the forces from Tlaxcala have ceased their war chants. Cortés is the first to speak.

CORTÉS (*Spanish*)
Are you not he? Are you not Motecuhzoma?

MALINCHE
Are you Motecuhzoma the Second? Are
you Motecuhzoma the Younger? Are you
the real one this time?

MOTECUHZOMA
It is so. I am he.

Motecuhzoma takes a step back. In amazement he beholds the strangers who have descended from the clouds. Even Cortés cannot hide his astonishment.

Motecuhzoma breaks the silence. His speech is serene, full of dignity, akin to prayer. However momentous, it utterly lacks rhetorical expression.

MOTECUHZOMA

Our lord, you are weary. The journey has
tired you, but now you are here on Earth.
You have come to your city, Mexico. You
have come to sit upon your throne, to sit
beneath your canopy. The kings who have
preceded me, likewise your custodians,
guarded your throne and preserved it for
your coming. They ruled for you, here in the
noble City of Mexico. The people were pro-
tected by their swords, and sheltered by their
shields. Do those kings know the destiny of
the ones left behind, their descendants? If
only they were watching, if only they could
marvel at what I see. No, it is not a dream.
I am not walking in my sleep. I do not dream
that I see you and look into your face. I have
met you, I have seen you at last! I was in
agony for five days, for ten days, with my
eyes fixed on the Region of Mystery. And
now you have come out of the mists and
clouds to sit on your throne once again. Rest
now, and take possession of your royal houses.
Welcome to your homeland, my lord.

Malinche has whispered the translation simultaneously to Cortés. He puts on his most genial face.

CORTÉS/MALINCHE

We have come to your house in the City of
Mexico. We feel a true abiding love for you.
We do. You have nothing to fear.

This time Cortés actually manages to pull off something like a fleeting embrace. He slaps Motecuhzoma on the back to assure him of his affection. Motecuhzoma recoils slightly: his death has touched him.

EXTERIOR. AXACAYATL'S PALACE. DAY.

Axacavatl's palace is located on the same central square where the Great Pyramid stands. Motecuhzoma's palace is diagonally across from it. In contrast to the otherwise flat buildings in the capital, both of these have an additional floor. They are expansive complexes containing a large number of halls, courtyards and chambers.

The Spanish procession and Motecuhzoma's escort cross the spacious square side by side, passing the ball court and the skull rack. The muffled thunder of a huge drum rumbles from atop the pyramid.

Cortés rides at the head of the procession with the Aztec ruler borne on his sedan chair beside him. Aztecs fill the square. A cloak spread out before Cortés' horse gets caught on a hoof, making the horse so nervous that his rider has to struggle to control him.

Covered with flowers, Motecuhzoma tosses a handful of petals unto Cortés.

> MOTECUHZOMA
> Master of Malinche, you are in your own
> house. So are your brethren. Do be at ease.

Malinche, behind Cortés, steps forth to quietly translate for him.

> MALINCHE (*low*)
> He means *you*, the lord of *me*. The empty
> palace of his father is where you'll reside.

Cortés nods pleasantly toward Motecuhzoma. Then he signals his marksmen to fire a salvo while marching along.

The enormous crowd is jolted as if it were one person. Even the emperor's sedan chair is jolted so hard that the flowers go flying in all directions. Slowly the dust and gunsmoke subside.

INTERIOR. AXACAYATL'S PALACE. DAY.

In rapid succession, several rooms, halls and interior court-yards. Everything is prepared for a regal reception. Flowers abound, mats on the floors, walls partly draped with weavings, trays of food neatly arrayed, and basins with incense.

FAST DISSOLVE TO

A grand interior courtyard. Spanish soldiers aim their positioned artillery at the entrance. No one has yet set down his weapons.

FAST DISSOLVE TO

A hall, into which the horses are led. A bed blanketed with flowers has been prepared for each horse.

FAST DISSOLVE TO

A sumptuous bedroom opening onto a courtyard has been reserved for Cortés. Above his bed is a feathered canopy. In one corner, a bed of flowers has been set for Cortés' horse. Okello holds the animal's reins with obvious unease.

Motecuhzoma, Cortés and Malinche are present, and a few servants who have laid out some fruit for them hasten away.

                    MALINCHE
          Their deer need corn to eat. It should be
          kept with the others. We also need carpen-
          ters. My lord wants a chapel constructed in
          the courtyard. Immediately.

MOTECUHZOMA
I shall send for them at once. But do ask
your master, the Prince of Turquoise, the
Rising Eagle, to be so kind as to order the
Tlaxcalans, our enemies, to leave the city.
Before they begin attacking my people.

Malinche confers momentarily with Cortés, then turns back
to the sovereign.

MALINCHE
The Tlaxcalans will camp on the mainland.
Trust us, Motecuhzoma. Take heart. We
love you very much.

INTERIOR. MOTECUHZOMA'S PALACE. NIGHT.

Motecuhzoma sits on a mat in the dark room lost in thought,
with just Cuitlahuac and Cuauhtemoc attending. Cuauhtemoc is quite aggravated, angrily pacing back and forth.

CUAUHTEMOC
The Tlaxcalans have not withdrawn – they
have taken refuge in the sacred inner courtyard. If these invaders are gods, then they
are gods who lie.

MOTECUHZOMA
We must watch them very carefully.

CUAUHTEMOC
We have been doing that ever since they first
appeared at the coast, and now they're here.

CUITLAHUAC
He's right.

CUAUHTEMOC
We should stop giving them food. If they're
really gods, then they don't live on fruit and
tortillas anyway.

CUITLAHUAC
He's absolutely right. We must get rid of them.

CUAUHTEMOC
We should attack them at once. They can't
escape. We'll remove the bridges from
the causeways, which will make them our
prisoners.

Motecuhzoma comes to life; this suggestion seems to go
much too far for him. But he's happy that someone in his
inner circle is so decisive.

MOTECUHZOMA
We'll cut off their provisions. Then, of
course, they'll *have* to withdraw.

EXTERIOR. AXACAYATL'S PALACE. MORNING.

A mute tension grips the morning scenery. Aztec scouts
and armed troops have taken positions all around the palace
where the foreigners are sequestered. The Aztecs seem to be
prepared for anything.

INTERIOR. AXACAYATL'S PALACE. MORNING.

The Spaniards are at their posts. All the muskets and crossbows are in place on the second floor. The horses stand
saddled in the main courtyard. Soldiers have donned their
armor, ready for all eventualities.

INTERIOR. AXACAYATL'S PALACE. DAY.

In an inner courtyard, Spanish soldiers wielding drawn
swords have forced a few Aztec servants to remove a round
stone tile from the floor. Cortés stands there, peering down
into the deep black shaft.

> CORTÉS
> *Un pozo*. I knew there would have to be a
> well here, somewhere.

Martín López, an older Spaniard with meaty hands and a
huge balding head, walks excitedly over to Cortés.

> LOPEZ (*Spanish*)
> *Capitán*, I may be just a carpenter, but I
> do understand a good deal about building
> construction. I believe I have discovered a
> hidden chamber –

INTERIOR. CORRIDOR IN AXACAYATL'S PALACE.
DAY.

A hallway lit by indirect daylight. Cortés, Lopez, Alvarado,
a few Spaniards and an Aztec servant gather. Lopez points
to a freshly whitewashed section of the wall, where the
vague shape of a door is discernible.

> LOPEZ (*Spanish*)
> It occurred to me that both rooms, left and
> right, are not as long as this corridor, mean-
> ing there must be a room in between. And,
> *here* – someone recently walled this area up.

Cortés looks around. Malinche isn't there. But he can find
out what he wants without translation. He who always
speaks in polished, courtly phrases suddenly grabs the
Aztec servant by the hair and drags him over to the freshly
painted part of the wall.

> CORTÉS (*Spanish*)
> What is behind there?

Cortés draws his sword and scratches the outline of the hidden door on the wall. The Aztec man he holds by the hair understands, but he cannot utter a word. He just trembles.

A few Spaniards have quickly broken a hole in the wall with axes and crowbars. Lopez peeks into the murky opening and recoils, incapable of any speech but a hesitant stutter.

> LOPEZ (*Spanish*)
> Th-there's g-*gold* in there!

Cortés looks inside and stiffens for a moment. Then he summons men over to instantly tear down the fresh wall. It crashes into the corridor in a wave of swirling dust.

P.O.V. SPANIARDS: THE SETTLING DUST.

In the dimness we can see a dazzling trove packed to the ceiling with vessels, masks, ornaments and chains, all made of gold, along with feathered crowns, obsidian knives, statues and ornate books. A treasure of incalculable value.

> CORTÉS (*Spanish*)
> Silence that servant immediately, once and
> for all. Seal the hidden chamber, as it was.

DISSOLVE TO

EXTERIOR. CAUSEWAY. DAY.

Bathed in bright golden sunlight, the mile-long causeway connecting the island of the capital city with the mainland. Not a soul is on it. Far away we see three figures approaching Tenochtitlan from somewhere abroad.

Three Spanish infantrymen rush toward the city. Exhausted and ragged, they seem to be coming from some distant place. One has a bandaged head, soaked with blood.

EXTERIOR. GRAND SQUARE IN TENOCHTITLAN.
DAY.

Cortés traverses the square with about thirty men. All his captains are with him, as well as Malinche and Aguilar, who, as is his wont, strides along naked but for his loincloth, and is the only unarmed man present.

Aztec warriors watch the proceedings from every rooftop.

INTERIOR. MOTECUHZOMA'S PALACE. DAY.

Motecuhzoma has surrounded himself with his highest officials. A lively discussion is under way; it stops when the Keeper of the House of Darkness enters. All eyes turn to him.

KEEPER
The Master of Malinche has come.
He wishes to pay our lord a visit.

NEZAHUALPILLI
Is he alone?

KEEPER
No.

CUAUHTEMOC
Then do not let him in.

Motecuhzoma seems amazed that decisions are being made over his head. He stiffens.

MOTECUHZOMA
I am the one who decides. Let my guests
come forth.

General bewilderment, but no one dares to contradict him
any further.

Cortés is quietly ushered in with his escort of several men.
Aguilar, wearing his loincloth, squats in a corner with some
palace servants. Cortés' face glows with geniality as he
doffs his hat and makes an elegant courtly bow to his host.
Motecuhzoma steps forward and sprinkles petals on him.

MOTECUHZOMA
Master of Malinche, I would like to give
you one of my daughters as a gift, as a gift
of delicious fruit.

Malinche translates softly to Cortés, then answers for him.

MALINCHE
My lord shall not accept this gift until your
daughter has accepted our faith.

MOTECUHZOMA
Is that truly what he wants?

Again she consults Cortés.

MALINCHE
He does want something else. May he speak
with you for a moment – alone?

Motecuhzoma casually waves his officials off, and they
reluctantly give way. Cortés confronts him at once and
surrounds the ruler with his armed men. An air of unease.
Glances seek glances; something seems a bit fishy. But the
conversation between the two leaders proceeds calmly,

almost whispered, although Cortés' tone has dramatically changed. Now his voice has a menacing ring.

CORTÉS/MALINCHE
Your allies have attacked our settlement on
the coast. They have captured one man and
wounded five. And they have sacrificed the
captive in their temple.

Motecuhzoma, remaining very quiet, immediately takes a defensive stance. This will be his undoing.

MOTECUHZOMA
How can that be?

MALINCHE
Three of our men escaped and found their
way to us. We know the attack had to have
been carried out at your command.

MOTECUHZOMA
I knew nothing of this.

Cortés communicates with his men with a single glance. Very gently and cautiously, the soldiers casually draw their swords.

CORTÉS (*Spanish*)
You are hereby ordered to come with me at
once.

Malinche instinctively decides to modify this into something more polite.

MALINCHE
My lord is willing to forgive you completely,
if you'll just come quietly to our quarters.

MOTECUHZOMA
I shall clear up this matter immediately, and
punish the guilty. Yes, I shall.

Wary of the drawn swords, he makes no move to come
along. Malinche looks for a sign from Cortés, who nods to
her almost imperceptibly. From this point on, whatever she
says seems to have been precisely orchestrated.

MALINCHE
If you make any noise, or put up any resis-
tance, my lord's officers will kill you on the
spot. That's the only reason they're here.

MOTECUHZOMA
My person is not such that can be taken
prisoner. Even if I would allow it, my
people never would.

Motecuhzoma looks around. The people in the hall have
clearly seen that something is wrong here. Anxiety is
rampant: there's sudden commotion at the door. Several
guards rush in.

Pedro de Alvarado takes a decisive step forward. With the
tip of his sword he touches the emperor's throat. Then he
mutters to his comrades.

ALVARADO (*Spanish*)
Why are we wasting time with all of this?
I'm for less talk and more *steel*. Either this
feathered hen comes with us or we skewer
his quivering flesh.

MOTECUHZOMA
What did he say?

MALINCHE
I would advise you to come with us. My
lord is unable to restrain his commanding
officers. They're very, very angry. And they
will not wait another minute.

INTERIOR. ANTEROOM OF HALL. DAY.

The Keeper of the House of Darkness arrives in the hall's
anteroom with a squad of palace guards. The warriors take
their positions.

EXTERIOR. GREAT SQUARE. DAY.

Feverish activity in the main square. Swarming Aztec warriors surround Motecuhzoma's palace from all directions,
while many others quickly encircle the Spanish quarters
across from it. The Spaniards take defensive positions on
their building's rooftop.

People flee into their houses. Children are swiftly evacuated
to safer places. Women clear out their market stands.

INTERIOR. GREAT HALL. DAY.

Cuauhtemoc, who has grasped the situation most acutely,
walks over to Motecuhzoma. At this critical moment, the
Spaniards close in with suicidal resolution. Everybody's life
is on the line.

CUAUHTEMOC
My lord, the palace guard is ready. We have
two thousand men outside. Shall I –

MOTECUHZOMA
No! Don't do anything! I will tell you when
I need you.

Abruptly putting a friendly expression back on his face, Cortés grabs Alvarado by the arm. Alvarado slowly lowers his sword, just a little.

> CORTÉS (*Spanish*)
> You can trust me. I am a man of honor. This will only take a short time.

> MALINCHE
> My lord would like you to come along with him only until the matter of the attack has been cleared up. He'll treat you with respect, and deal with you honorably. He loves you like the brother you are to him. Everything will be just like it always is – you can easily conduct your business of state from our quarters, and do it as well there as anywhere.

> MOTECUHZOMA
> I'll give you my two eldest sons as hostages. They will be –

> MALINCHE
> *Enough*. No more delays. My lord does love you, but his officers are extremely angry. They have decided against him.

It hasn't escaped Cuauhtemoc that the Spaniards, in collusion with Malinche, are acting out a well-plotted scheme.

> CUAUHTEMOC
> My lord will not go with you.

> MOTECUHZOMA
> Silence! I would like to demonstrate my good will. Everything can be clarified quite simply: our guests were assaulted at the coast, and now the guilty ones shall be

brought to justice here at once. Bring them
to me this very instant! And bring my sedan
chair.

A deathly hush sets in. Swords remain pointed at Motecuhzoma. Old Nezahualpilli, the far-sighted one, breaks the
silence.

NEZAHUALPILLI
Lord, if you follow them, you will never
know freedom again. You will die a captive.

CLOSE-UP: MOTECUHZOMA'S FACE SLOWLY
TRANSFORMED BY RAPTURE.

Motecuhzoma is lost in a distant vision. He somehow needs
to escape reality.

MOTECUHZOMA
We only came to sleep.
We only came to dream.
It is not true.
No, it is not true.
That we came to live on earth.

A moment of silence. No one knows just what will come
next. To everyone's surprise, squatting Aguilar speaks.

AGUILAR
These are my people now. I'm staying here
with them. I'm not moving anywhere.

Silence. This deviation from the script embarrasses the
Spaniards.

AGUILAR
Not one inch.

EXTERIOR. TENOCHTITLAN, GREAT SQUARE. DAY.

Motecuhzoma is borne in his sedan across the great square by high-ranking officials. The Spanish troops are pressing in around him, ready for anything extreme. Other top Aztec officials, women and servants follow.

> AGUILAR (O.S.)
> *Ni una pulgada!* Not one inch!

To the rear, roughly clutched by Spanish soldiers who push and shove him toward their quarters, defiant Aguilar rages in his loincloth.

Alvarado has the point of his sword at the emperor's throat for all to see. He only needs a little push to kill him.

From a distance we see the procession move through thronged Aztec warriors poised for action. Extreme tension hovers over the square. Nothing happens. Then the sudden blown blast of a conch shell resounds from the Great Temple, and a mountainous drum joins in with a slow, ominous, rumbling drone. This towering, overpowering, unrelenting sound may never abate.

INTERIOR. SPANISH QUARTERS, MOTECUHZOMA'S ROOM. DAY.

Motecuhzoma's new room. A spacious chamber in the Spanish quarters, leading out to a small floral courtyard. Everything seems makeshift, even the emperor's canopied throne and mat. Otherwise the room seems bare.

A few officers of the court crouch by a wall. Servants, guards; a young woman hands the emperor his long, clay, tobacco-filled pipe.

Motecuhzoma smokes, lost in thought. The others leave him to his solitude.

INTERIOR. CORRIDOR IN SPANISH QUARTERS. DAY.

The entrance to Motecuhzoma's chamber. Spanish guards are stationed here with drawn swords, loaded muskets, and a light field artillery piece manned by a vigilant cannoneer. He has a basin with glowing coals beside him, so he can light the fuse at any time.

EXTERIOR. COURTYARD. DAY.

A small contingent of Spanish guards, at their posts in the enclosed courtyard. A tiny monkey clambers over a young soldier's crossbow.

INTERIOR. SPANISH QUARTERS, MOTECUH-ZOMA'S ROOM. DAY.

Cortés enters with Malinche. He removes his hat with a grandiose flourish, bowing deeply in strict accordance with Spanish court etiquette. He does not replace his hat on his head, but holds it over his heart.

> CORTÉS (*Spanish*)
> My brother!

Motecuhzoma barely comes to life, but ignores this greeting.

> CORTÉS (*Spanish*)
> See if he knows that we have found the gold.

> MALINCHE
> My lord has discovered the hidden gold in here, in your father's palace.

Motecuhzoma stares off after his tobacco smoke.

                    MOTECUHZOMA
          I am aware of that.

                    MALINCHE
          Is there more in your palace? My lord needs
          more. He has –

Cortés, who has understood without translation, interrupts.

                    CORTÉS (*Spanish*)
          My men are suffering from a disease for
          which the only cure is gold.

He smiles his most genial smile. Malinche grasps its meaning.

                    MALINCHE
          He asks that you accompany him to the next
          room.

INTERIOR. ROOM IN SPANISH QUARTERS. DAY.

A completely emptied room: whitewashed, clean, freshly
swept. Motecuhzoma stands with Malinche in the middle of
the cell, watching Cortés scratch a line around the four walls
as high as he can reach with the tip of his sword.

                    MALINCHE
          My lord will restore your freedom and leave
          in peace if you fill this room with gold.
          Until then, he'll have no other choice but to
          keep looking out for your safety here.

Cortés slips his sword back into its sheath and steps over to
Motecuhzoma. He embraces him, and conveys the warmest
expression of his affection with a kiss of brotherhood.

CORTÉS (*Spanish*)
My friend. My dear, dear friend. *Brother.*

He declares this with his most grandiose, operatic elegance. Too paralyzed by the situation to do anything about it, Motecuhzoma simply lets it happen.

EXTERIOR. ROOF OF SPANISH QUARTERS. DAY.

The flat roof of the whitewashed palace of Axacayatl in the blazing sunlight.

Motecuhzoma walks over to a low balustrade at the roof's edge. Alvarado stands behind him, his hand squeezing the handle of his drawn sword. Six of his soldiers stand with him, ready for action. Two marksmen aim their cocked weapons directly at Motecuhzoma.

P.O.V. MOTECUHZOMA: THE MAIN SQUARE, AND HIS PALACE BEYOND.

The square is eerily empty save for a handful of Aztecs, standing motionless. An earthly stillness. Aztec warriors are positioned on every rooftop.

CLOSE-UP: MOTECUHZOMA'S FACE RADIATES A MELANCHOLIC DIGNITY.

MOTECUHZOMA
Mexicans! Where are you? Your sovereign
speaks! Hear me now: fetch my crown
treasures, and fetch the treasures from the
sacred chambers of the gods. Your sovereign
shall soon be with you once again! And hear
this: bring provisions for our guests. Bring
tamales, turkeys, fruit and corn. And bring
grass for their deer!

An eerie, vacuous hush on the square below. The few who stand there do not move. An old man among them mumbles something in opposition.

MOTECUHZOMA
Our god speaks forth from my mouth!

OLD MAN
He has lived on the lake for forty years and knows *nothing* of frogs.

Down on the square, the deflated few withdraw. They leave the square alone, but for the shame of its nakedness.

INTERIOR. SPANISH QUARTERS, MOTECUHZOMA'S ROOM. NIGHT.

Motecuhzoma's room in Axacayatl's palace is torchlit. A few basins with glowing coals add tufts of warm amber light. The air is cold.

Motecuhzoma has gathered his brother, his nephew, King Nezahualpilli and the Keeper of the House of Darkness around him. All of them have wrapped themselves tightly in their coarse, humble cloaks.

The emperor cowers on his throne in his gold-tressed feather cloak. His visitors warm their hands on mugs filled with foaming hot chocolate.

Beyond them, a squad of Spanish guards, their number increased because of the visitors. Malinche is near them supervising the servants, repeatedly sending women to replenish the glowing coals, or copal, or get fresh chocolate.

It is obvious to everyone that the purpose of Malinche's presence is to monitor all that's being said. But to sustain the illusion of a normal, undisturbed meeting of the Crown Council, she remains a respectful distance from it.

Cuitlahuac has taken the floor in a thoroughly businesslike manner.

> CUITLAHUAC
> The lord of the city of Chalco has died.
> Who shall succeed him?

> MOTECUHZOMA
> Pinoti.

> CUITLAHUAC
> And who shall be appointed the new judge
> in Texcoco?

Motecuhzoma is ever taciturn. The group sticks strictly to business, but seems to await some sort of cue, some opportunity.

> MOTECUHZOMA
> Xochitl. The elder.

> CUAUHTEMOC
> Isn't he too old?

> MOTECUHZOMA
> The city needs an experienced man.

Cuauhtemoc discreetly eyes Malinche, who is busy with some servants.

> CUAUHTEMOC (*low*)
> Some of the invaders intend to journey up
> to the top of the volcano. We ought to let
> them, and show them *they* are the ones in
> captivity.

He notices that Malinche is eavesdropping now. Trading glances with his peers, he continues in a louder voice, assuming a business-as-usual tone.

CUAUHTEMOC
What Texcoco needs most is a young, vigor-
ous judge. I propose Xochitl's son.

From the corner of his eye, Cuauhtemoc sees that Malinche
is distracted again.

CUAUHTEMOC (*low*)
*We must show them our strength. We have
to.*

Motecuhzoma plays along with him. As if referring to the
appointment of a new judge in Texcoco, he supports his
nephew in a bold, decisive tone of voice.

MOTECUHZOMA
Very well, I agree. Let the younger man
prevail.

With that he nods toward Cuauhtemoc.

EXTERIOR. TENOCHTITLAN, MAIN SQUARE.
MORNING.

The central square is deserted, yet on all the roofs and
accessways we can see Aztec warriors set to strike. An air of
suspense blankets the city. The dull thud of the mammoth
drum continues to resound from the Great Pyramid. It adds
an oppressive sense to the dim, desolate square, gray with
the yawning of dawn.

A line of porters approaches from Motecuhzoma's
palace, and a second file advances from the direction of the
square. The two lines meet in the middle to form a double
file, which now proceeds toward Axacayatl's palace.

A few high officials supervise the porters as the Keeper of
the House of Darkness, who leads the procession, is carried
forward on a simple sedan chair.

EXTERIOR. ROOM IN SPANISH QUARTERS. MORNING.

Motecuhzoma and Cortés are standing by the doorway to the previously empty room, now half-filled with gold. Various vessels, goblets, jewelry, bracelets, earlobe and lip pegs, indiscriminately stacked and strewn all over.

In the middle of the room, Malinche watches Alvarado check the opened bundles for gold, eliminating all else. He disposes of the jade, plucks feathers from gold objects, and tosses aside garments merely embroidered in gold.

> MALINCHE
> We said *gold*! And nothing *but*! Don't
> bother us with anything else!

The porters assess Alvarado's vandalism with dismay. Motecuhzoma cannot bear to witness what is happening to his most precious treasures.

> MOTECUHZOMA
> Master of Malinche, you have asked that
> some of my porters accompany your
> brothers who wish to climb the volcano, for
> what reason I don't know. I would like to
> send my nephew, Cuauhtemoc, with them
> as well. He's young and very strong. In any
> case, one of my magicians shall go along.

Malinche translates for Cortés, who only has eyes for the gold and very little patience for this subject of discussion.

> CORTÉS (*Spanish*)
> A magician? Why a magician?

> MALINCHE
> Why is this? What for?

MOTECUHZOMA
To reconcile the spirits of the mountain. The
mountain is sacred. No one is allowed to
climb it. *No one.* People who climb mountains lose all reason.

Malinche translates. Cortés seems unwilling to respond.
Things are going too slowly for him; he has no time for this.
Malinche tries to add something to clarify the matter.

MALINCHE
But those huge irons of ours that spew fire
and thunder need fresh nourishment.

That seems to satisfy Motecuhzoma. He wants to discuss
something else.

MOTECUHZOMA
The room shall be filled today. I must be
back in my palace by nightfall.

Malinche briefly confers again with Cortés.

MALINCHE
Not until you have turned those assailants
from the coast over to my lord.

EXTERIOR. SPANISH QUARTERS, COURTYARD.
DAY.

Alvarado drives two of the porters ahead of him into the
open courtyard, where feathers and garments have been
piled high for burning. The fire gives off a great deal of
smoke, but has trouble staying aflame. Two cursing Spaniards poke the shafts of their lances around in the heap to
stoke the smoldering valuables.

The porters, who are weeping, toss more feathers and fabrics into the flames, where we also see ornate pictorial texts and holy scriptures.

EXTERIOR. CAUSEWAY. DAY.

Alvarado leads a small group of soldiers taking this causeway out of town. With them are Cuauhtemoc and nine Aztec porters. Armed only with lances and halberds, the Spaniards wear no armor. The porters carry strikingly large rolls of rope and buckets. The Imperial Magician is among them.

The contingent crosses a wooden bridge. Waiting Aztecs remove the bridge the moment the last man steps off it. Whoever remains in Tenochtitlan can be effortlessly cut off from the mainland; this seems to be the point of the Aztecs' maneuver. Alvarado notes this with indifference, no matter how grave its limpid meaning: *There will be no escaping across the lake in case of open conflict.*

EXTERIOR. MOUNTAIN PASS. DAY.

Cuauhtemoc and the magician have stayed behind on the high pass between the two volcanoes. The small expedition has traveled a fair distance, and works its way slowly up the mountain.

> MAGICIAN
> Go no further. The vile kings who have died
> live in this mountain. And be warned: they
> will make the earth beneath you quiver.

> CUAUHTEMOC
> Let's go up there. We have to see what the
> strangers' intentions are. Come on.

He ascends the slope, following the tracks that the climbers ahead have left in the char-gray ash.

EXTERIOR. BIVOUAC. NIGHT.

A small campfire in the night. The howling wind flattens its flames. Spanish soldiers and Aztec porters huddled close-ly around the fire warm themselves against the icy cold, wrapped in woolen blankets. Only their eyes glow from the reflection of the flames.

MED. CLOSE-UP: ALVARADO AND CUAUHTE-MOC ARE SITTING BODY-TO-BODY, IN THEIR EFFORT TO KEEP EACH OTHER WARM.

A short, silent, ineffable moment of elemental harmony, as snow begins to flurry. Alvarado breathes puffed gusts that instantly freeze. His moustache has become an ingot of ice.

> ALVARADO (*Spanish*)
> There must be sulfur up there. But there is
> more than that. No man has ever been up
> there before.

As Alvarado points toward the summit, Cuauhtemoc misconstrues this.

> CUAUHTEMOC
> Yes, of course. Those vile, salamander kings
> way up in there grovel by day, and ravage
> by night.

EXTERIOR. GLACIER. DAY.

Glacial ice, deep crevices, icy wind. The air is crystal clear. Laboriously, the expedition trudges up the mountain. The peak is enshrouded by clouds, which quickly engulf the men.

Spanish soldiers poke their lances into the ice, digging out little steps to walk on with their boots and hands. Alvarado slams his halberd into the glacier and works his way up by the handle, gasping for breath.

The Indians have sandals on their bare feet. It seems inconceivable that they have climbed this high in the ice without boots.

EXTERIOR. POPOCATEPETL. DAY.

We are now at an altitude of 17,900 feet. Alvarado has reached the ice-lipped mouth of the crater, which emits a muffled growl while white and sulfurous-yellow smoke wells up and billows forth from within. His probing eyes search for a vista, but they only see smoke and clouds.

The small exhausted group joins him at the peak. The Aztecs have changed their technique: the front man has wedged himself firmly into the ice and holds a rope, which the others clutch as they climb.

EXTERIOR. CRATER. DAY.

Cuauhtemoc has descended into the crater with some of the porters. Dense smoke comes billowing up at them. Now we see the purpose of the ropes: the porters use them to lower the buckets into the growling pit and bring them back up with yellow, smoking sulfur.

A plummeting bucket disappears down into the fuming funnel. Alvarado carefully inspects the smoking yellow poison bubbling in another bucket. He seems satisfied. A hissing gust of smoke snorts from the depths.

EXTERIOR. SPANISH QUARTERS, COURTYARD. TWILIGHT.

Dusk. The little flowered courtyard that is part of Motecuhzoma's new quarters. A few Spanish guards stand unobtrusively to the rear.

Motecuhzoma and Cortés sit facing each other on their collapsible Moorish chairs. Malinche attends behind Cortés. A pensive air, a silent pause.

MOTECUHZOMA
It's like some peculiar dream. I am *your*
captive, and you in turn are *my* captive.

MALINCHE
My lord knows that.

Another short pause. Something is seething in Cortés.

CORTÉS (*Spanish*)
Is this country Mexico an island? I'm told
that the ocean continues in the West. How
big is this island?

MALINCHE
My lord wishes to know if this is an island.

MOTECUHZOMA
This is no *island.* This is the earthly *world.*

Malinche briefly confers with Cortés.

MALINCHE/CORTÉS
I have already concluded that, from the
height of the mountains, the size of the
rivers, and the number of tongues. Now,
I would like to make a proposal to you.

Motecuhzoma nods to Cortés.

MALINCHE/CORTÉS
You have many enemies. The nations you
once conquered are rebelling. *If* you embrace the only True God, and *if* you declare
yourself a subject of His Imperial Majesty,
the great and invincible Emperor Charles, I
would like to embark upon a military cam-
paign, in partnership with you, to conquer all
of India and China. *Then* you would be free.

MOTECUHZOMA

"*India*," what is that? And "*China*," what
is *that*? And who is this Emperor Charles?
Ours is a good and godly world. Our
enemies have been conquered. There is no
"*India*."

EXTERIOR. SPANISH QUARTERS, COURTYARD.
TWILIGHT.

The spacious, almost vacant inner courtyard of Axacayatl's
palace. The Spanish force has established a kind of field
camp here. Cannons in position. Saddled horses in a corner,
munching fresh grass. Sentries on the roof.

In the middle of the courtyard, the Spaniards have set up a
foundry. Glowing fire, bellows, an iron smelting mold on
the end of a pole. A tall stack of gold objects is being melted
down into bars.

Cortés and Alvarado quietly oversee this. A notary accounts
for each item.

CLOSE-UP: EXQUISITE GOLD NECKLACE WITH
SHELLS AND FROGS LIQUEFIES IN THE SMELT-
ING PAN.

Motecuhzoma leans against a column in the arcaded courtyard, watching his very culture melt away. Tears stream
down his cheeks.

MOTECUHZOMA

Does nothing ever return from the Realm
of Wonder? Does no one return from the
No-Returning? As a song you were born,
my people.

Alvarado arrives with a porter and a load of gold. He listens
momentarily, comprehending nothing.

ALVARADO (*Spanish*)
Sure. Of course. How right you are.

EXTERIOR. TENOCHTITLAN, GREAT SQUARE. DAY.

The stand-off between the besieged Spaniards and the Aztecs continues. Marksmen lie in position on the roof of the Spanish quarters. The surrounding roofs are manned by Indians brandishing spears, arrows and slings. All access roads to the square have been blocked by their fellow warriors.

A cluster of servants rushes across the square. They drop packages of provisions by an entrance to the invaders' quarters and immediately dash off.

INTERIOR. SPANISH QUARTERS, MOTECUHZO-MA'S ROOM. NIGHT.

Flickering amber light, drifting wisps of smoke, an intimate air in the imprisoned king's quarters. Cortés, Motecuhzoma, Malinche. An ocelot sleeps on a cushion beside the emperor. Watchful Spanish guards lurk in shadows behind them.

Seated opposite each other on low stools, with a low table between them, Motecuhzoma contemplates his game of patolli with Cortés, who has a chessboard and chessmen before him.

[The Aztec game of patolli consists of a cross-shaped board with stems divided into fifty-two fields, upon which the players move stones or beans, according to the roll of the "dice." These "dice" are small, halved sections of bamboo with symbols inscribed in the hollow of the concave side, whereas the upraised side is blank. When tossed, they fall on either their "back" or their "face." The game is vaguely reminiscent of backgammon.]

The atmosphere is betrayed by an undercurrent of appre-
hension. As he explains the rules of the game, Motecuhzoma strives to defuse the tension.

> MOTECUHZOMA
> Since we are the only two players, the two of
> us must pretend to be four.

> CORTÉS (*Spanish*)
> And there is Malinche. Can we play with
> three?

> MOTECUHZOMA
> Yes, it would be possible. But we should
> keep it to the two of us. Each of us will have
> his shadow man. The god Quetzalcoatl is
> mine.

Malinche translates. Cortés' tone changes a bit, being more
serious than before.

> CORTÉS (*Spanish*)
> Mine is the crown, the king of Spain.

> MOTECUHZOMA
> Instead of having three stones to move, each
> of us will have six. And we'll each have four
> pieces of half-reed, which are used much
> like the dice I see your guards use.

He tosses the half-reeds, his "dice," and instantly places his
stones on the board with astonishing speed.

> MOTECUHZOMA
> Fifteen.

> CORTÉS/MALINCHE
> *Fifteen?* How did you calculate that?

Motecuhzoma lines up his four "dice" on the table. He offers a very businesslike explanation to Cortés.

> MOTECUHZOMA
> What's most important is whether the blank back or the inscribed face is up.

CLOSE-UP: THE FOUR HALF-REED, BAMBOO "DICE."

> MOTECUHZOMA
> The backs are nothing. Now two faces show a ring. Each counts as one. The checkered flag over there is fifteen. The last one with the full flag, that counts as twenty. So the face value of these half-reeds is one, one, fifteen and twenty.

He places three "dice" with backs up, then adds one face-up, revealing its ring symbol.

> MOTECUHZOMA
> Zero. Zero. Zero. And the ring is one. So everything together comes to *one.*

Cortés thinks he understands. He turns a zero over, showing the full flag.

> CORTÉS/MALINCHE
> Zero. Zero. The "one" stays, plus the "twenty." So it all adds up to *twenty-one.*

> MOTECUHZOMA
> Not so: two. We are still in the unoccupied parts, in the "Weak Fields." Only from here...

He gestures quickly toward the crux of the stems, and to the four "turning points" at the tip of each stem.

MOTECUHZOMA
Only from the "Strong Fields" is the stones'
imprisonment lifted. As it is with me. From
now on, then, the following is in effect –

Slowly Motecuhzoma overturns a half-reed with the ring
symbol.

CORTÉS
One.

MOTECUHZOMA
I am in the Strong Fields, and the dice count
differently now.

Motecuhzoma flips over the next half-reed.

CORTÉS (*Spanish*)
Again, *one*. Together that makes *two*.

Now Motecuhzoma assumes a more serious tone of voice.

MOTECUHZOMA
Master of Malinche, what would happen if
you killed me?

He overturns the next half-reed to the symbol worth
fifteen. Cortés bites his lip. He seems to have toyed with the
same thought.

CORTÉS (*Spanish*)
Fifteen. But I would never do that. Fifteen
plus two makes seventeen. I would never
kill you. *Never.* Because I love you, like my
brother, like my very own blood.

Motecuhzoma levels with Cortés.

MOTECUHZOMA

Isn't it true that if you killed me, you and
all of your men would perish? Isn't it?
Am I not in the Strong Fields? It's you
who is now in a foreign country. It's *you*
who's trapped on an island, with all bridges
removed. It's you, with your four hundred
men, who have been surrounded by two
hundred thousand of my bravest warriors.
You. You would no longer have food to eat,
you know. Nor would your deer.

Cortés becomes very blunt.

CORTÉS (*Spanish*)

If I choose to look at it this way, you as my
prisoner are worth something to me only if
I keep you alive. But –

MOTECUHZOMA

But are you not *my* prisoner, as well?

CORTÉS (*Spanish*)

– but that is not how *I* see it.

Impasse. Motecuhzoma loses himself in thought.

MOTECUHZOMA

Is my god weary of me? Has he lost faith in
me? Why has he brought alien beings here?
Who are you, to come like an eagle from
the end of the earth, with no respect for the
old or young? Why have you destroyed so
many of us? Why won't you stop until we
are humbled, cowed, defeated?

CORTÉS (*Spanish*)

I cannot stop. How could I? If I left you
here untouched, and you promised to let

me go, I wouldn't reach the coast alive,
because your warriors would kill me. They
would kill me because I would seem to be
fleeing. If I did reach the coast, my own
people would come in enormous numbers
to punish me and conquer Mexico anyway.
I couldn't possibly hold them back, I could
never keep them from coming. My fate is
clear: even if I would want to stop, I can
stop no more. I know my fate.

MOTECUHZOMA
As I know mine. Yes, you will move on.
You have come here as an intruder.

CORTÉS (*Spanish*)
He who comes not by the front door, comes
as a thief.

Looking into each other's eyes, the two men are embarrassed by their openness. Motecuhzoma turns over the last of the "dice" with its full flag upraised, representing twenty.

CORTÉS (*Spanish*)
We left off with two, plus fifteen, which is
seventeen. So seventeen and twenty makes
thirty-seven.

MOTECUHZOMA
Not so. *Five.* When thrown in one toss,
it makes five.

CORTÉS (*Spanish*)
I have no idea how you Mexicans count.

MOTECUHZOMA
I know how *you* count. We count beans
that way. Otherwise all our numbers are
different. They have a very deep *resonance.*

In each of them the gods dwell, as they do
in the cycles of the universe. Your numbers
are stark and naked and void. They have no
resonance, no meaning at all.

CLOSE-UP: THE STERN FACES OF MOTECUHZO-
MA AND CORTÉS, EYE TO EYE.

MOTECUHZOMA
Now you show me *your* game.

Cortés places his chess board in the middle of the table, its
pieces already in their proper positions.

CORTÉS (*Spanish*)
Each of us has a set of pieces, like armies
facing each other. Each piece is moved
differently. These two are the kings – the
goal of the game is to kill the opponent's
king. A pawn moves like this, a bishop
like this, the knights like this, the queens
go there and there and there, and then the
castles.

Cortés sets a few of his pieces forward against Motecuhzoma's opposing ranks and allows his adversary time to pon-
der the configuration on the board. Motecuhzoma responds
quite unexpectedly: he quickly rearranges his pieces into
two parallel blocks, with a gap between them.

CORTÉS (*Spanish*)
But you can't do that. The rules of the game
allow just one piece to be moved at a time.

MOTECUHZOMA
I haven't moved them yet. This is simply
how my army prepares for battle. So *move*.
You go first.

Motecuhzoma slides one of Cortés' "men" into the gap, dividing his pieces.

MOTECUHZOMA
See? Do you see that? You would be trapped.

Cortés is too bewildered to even attempt to correct him.

EXTERIOR. CENTRAL SQUARE. SUNRISE.

Dawn's light graces the top of the Great Pyramid and the roofs of the buildings. We make out nervous movements of the Aztec warriors manning the rooftops.

REINFORCEMENTS arrive. A tense, apprehensive atmosphere.

INTERIOR. SPANISH QUARTERS, CORTÉS' HALL. DAY.

Cortés on his Moorish seat beneath the canopy. All his officers are assembled, along with armed soldiers. A group of Indian prisoners has been thrown to the floor at Cortés' feet. These captives are in awful shape. Apart from wrist and ankle irons, they are attached to one another by chains linked to neck irons.

Alvarado pushes more than escorts Motecuhzoma into the room. Cortés promptly unwraps a bloody cloth covering something. The bearded, severed head of a Spaniard is revealed.

CORTÉS (*Spanish*)
You have betrayed me. You have lied to me.
You have deceived me. And this is no game.

Malinche continues alone.

MALINCHE
This is one of my master's brothers. They
ripped out his heart while it was still beating, and sacrificed him. Now even though
we are pleased that you have turned the
renegades over to us –

MOTECUHZOMA
And surely they said I knew nothing of this –

MALINCHE
– their leader has just *confessed.*

Malinche turns and briefly mutters something to Alvarado,
who gives the most battered of the brutally beaten men on
the floor a vicious kick. The unfortunate man, Qualpopoca,
struggles to right himself.

MALINCHE
Who gave the orders?

QUALPOPOCA
My lord and ruler: Motecuhzoma.

MOTECUHZOMA
But that's not true, Qualpopoca – you know
that!

Malinche whispers a quick word to Cortés who, aware that
the man's confession had been coerced, springs to his feet,
screaming in feigned agitation.

CORTÉS (*Spanish*)
Aha! He even knows his name!

Furious, Cortés continues his raving harangue as Malinche
translates over him.

CORTÉS/MALINCHE
You are a *traitor*! You have rebelled against
His Majesty, the Emperor of Spain! I hereby
command my officers to publicly burn the
murderers at the stake, and that you be
clamped in irons and forced to bear witness
to this!

MOTECUHZOMA
But, Malinche –

CORTÉS (*Spanish*)
Don't call me Malinche!

MALINCHE
And don't call him Master of Malinche.

CLOSE-UP: MOTECUHZOMA EYES MALINCHE,
CORTÉS.

MOTECUHZOMA
Hernán Cortés.

Corte stares him down icily.

CORTÉS
Don Hernán Cortés.

Alvarado and four Spanish soldiers seize the Emperor of
Mexico. He only emits an inaudible yelp. Then, in deep
shock, Motecuhzoma lets them clamp heavy irons on him.

EXTERIOR. TENOCHTITLAN, GREAT SQUARE.
MORNING.

A pyre has been erected in the middle of the main square,
surrounded by a rectangular formation of almost all the
Spanish troops.

The Spaniards, their backs to the pyre, aim their weapons at the Aztecs – the few who are there, perhaps two hundred – who have anxiously withdrawn to the square's periphery. Numerous observers are hiding from view on rooftops all around. Warriors wait along the roads leading to the square, ready to intervene. No one dares do anything.

The prisoners from the coast are bound to stakes above the pyre. Father Olmedo sprinkles them with holy water.

An armed squad of elite soldiers led by Cortés emerges from the Spanish quarters. In their midst is Motecuhzoma. Swords point at him as massive attack dogs bark and snarl and bare their teeth at him. They can barely be held back on their leashes.

Motecuhzoma slowly moves along, his leg irons allowing only small steps. He has an iron manacle around his neck, and Alvarado leads him like a dog on a leash. The Aztec emperor holds his head high. He reveals a dignity that endures beyond death.

A scream from countless thousands of throats arises from the roofs and streets and houses of Tenochtitlan. A few lamenting voices notwithstanding, the sound is the sound of wrath.

At the pyre, Alvarado torches the bundles of kindling wood. Olmedo starts chanting the Te Deum. The Spaniards sing along, but are shouted down by the Aztecs' fury. It's as if the entire world is in a state of rage.

INTERIOR. SPANISH QUARTERS, COURTYARD. DAY.

To assuage the shock from the public display of the shackled emperor at the execution, Aguilar removes Motecuhzoma's leg irons.

MOTECUHZOMA
Why have they sent *you* to unshackle me?

AGUILAR
I'm not sure. But the captain knows that
you're fond of me.

Busy with the leg irons, Aguilar looks up at Motecuhzoma.

MOTECUHZOMA
Why are they doing this to me? Don't they
have the nerve to kill me right away? Would
they really take my heart but make me stay?

AGUILAR
I don't know.

MOTECUHZOMA
But you are the one who would know.

AGUILAR
No, I'm really no longer one of them. After
my shipwreck, the people at the coast kept
me in captivity for eight long years, and
I never believed I would ever be rescued.
So I lived the life of a Maya and learned
their language, and by the time the captain
found me, the only thing in Spanish I could
remember was "Toledo."

MOTECUHZOMA
What is that?

AGUILAR
The city I come from.

MOTECUHZOMA
But still, you must know them better than I.

AGUILAR
I think I still know them, and I think I
know you. But only one thing is absolutely
certain, something no one who comes after
us will ever understand: you are the one
person who can save this city. Only you can
save it. Only you can atone. You and you
alone.

INTERIOR. SPANISH QUARTERS, MOTECUHZO-
MA'S ROOM. EVENING.

The twilight of the flowered courtyard sheds an elega-
ic glow into Motecuhzoma's room. The Crown Council
is assembled. And, as always, Spanish guards attend. But
Malinche is missing; no one seems to be spying this time on
Motecuhzoma's conference with his most trusted advisors.

Motecuhzoma has aged visibly. He takes the floor.

MOTECUHZOMA
The high priests have discussed with me an
even more disturbing possibility.

CUITLAHUAC
Which is –

MOTECUHZOMA
Which is that the Master of Malinche is not
our god Quetzalcoatl at all, but, rather, he's
Tezcatlipoca – the Smoking Mirror. This is
the god who has enjoyed cheating people
out of their homes and all they own, who
has mocked and ridiculed men, has quick-
ened vice and sin. This is a god of anguish,
and affliction, who has brought all things
down.

NEZAHUALPILLI
I can see a far worse possibility, that –

MOTECUHZOMA
That what?

Old Nezahualpilli hesitates, which isn't his usual way of doing things.

NEZAHUALPILLI
That the Master of Malinche and his
invaders are *humans* – and, much worse
yet, that they will annihilate us all. I know
that's their sole objective.

Motecuhzoma's inner circle cautiously agrees. These men obviously have mulled this over already.

MOTECUHZOMA
Whatever they are, I must speak now of
myself: I have become a burden to Mexico,
one it needn't bear. Cuauhtemoc, if I were
dead you could use our warriors to deal
with this, as you have always demanded.
Your noble restraint has been in consider-
ation of my safety, and I'm terribly grateful
for your loyalty and love. But now I wish
to die. To cross over into the Realm of the
Dark Emptiness. This is the only wish I
have.

Cuauhtemoc is profoundly distressed; he refuses to agree with this. But he does something uniquely unusual, some-thing forbidden: he extends his hand and lays it on the hand of the Untouchable One. Everyone present is witnessing what has never been witnessed before.

CLOSE-UP: CUITLAHUAC, NEZAHUALPILLI AND KEEPER OF HOUSE OF DARKNESS.

CUITLAHUAC

O lord, your wish is utterly out of the
question; the thought of it alone would be
unbearable for us. You are the One Who
Commands. You are the Heart of our city,
you are the sacred Quetzal Feather, a wall,
a barricade, in the shadow of which our
people find refuge. Your word is precious
jade. You speak in the name of the gods,
whose seat and whose voice you are.

CUAUHTEMOC

The same gods who not only require you to
rule over Mexico, but to keep the universe
alive.

KEEPER

You have been deified. Although you're
human, as we are, although you're our
friend, although you're our son, you're no
longer human: the god speaks from your
mouth.

MOTECUHZOMA

I shall soon die, the same way any human dies.

EXTERIOR. GREAT PYRAMID. DAY.

Motecuhzoma and Cortés climb the Great Pyramid. Both
leaders spurn all offers of aid in ascending the steep stairway.
Spanish soldiers clamber up to the left and right of them, ready
to kill the Aztec ruler if he makes the slightest move to break
free.

As always, the warriors are in position on rooftops surrounding the pyramid. As always, the dull rumble of the
monstrous drum. Upon reaching the top, Motecuhzoma
falls silent. Malinche is there, awaiting Cortés.

MOTECUHZOMA
So, yes, I'm here. I wanted to stand on this
pyramid one last time.

Malinche passes this along to Cortés as he pauses beside her,
discreetly taking her hand. For a moment he's mystified.

CORTÉS/MALINCHE
Why one last time? I merely intend to
destroy these hideous idols. And to install
an icon of our Blessed Virgin holding her
Most Precious Son. But I order you first
to forbid all further human sacrifice and to
renounce Satan. After that I'll come here
every morning with you to pray.

Motecuhzoma steps before Cortés and opens his feathered
cloak. His body is naked but for a gold-embroidered loincloth and a jade chain around his neck. He takes Cortés'
hand and places it on his bronze chest.

MOTECUHZOMA
Master of Malinche, my people look upon
me as a god, but touch me – I'm no such
thing. I'm actually a father of fifty-two
children, and a prisoner. I have no power to
stop you.

Malinche has quietly translated. Cortés pulls his hand back.

CORTÉS (*Spanish*)
No heart can possibly beat in there as long as
you sacrifice human beings.

MALINCHE
My lord wishes to know why you sacrifice
human beings.

MOTECUHZOMA

It's the most precious gift we humans can
offer our gods. Every night, the Sun God
fights the Demons of Darkness, and our
meek souls are filled with the fear that
the Sun might be defeated. *Human blood
nourishes the Sun*. It restores her power to
rise on high once again, and thus it keeps
the universe circling. As for our wars, we
have never fought a war to destroy others;
we call them Wars of Flowers, since our sole
aim is to take prisoners, whom we sacrifice.
These captives are unafraid – they know
that they're messengers to the gods, and that
the death they must die shall honor them.

CORTÉS (*Spanish*)

No man may take another's life in God's
name. I order you to take instructions in
our faith and its mystery at once, guided by
the hand of our most pious *padre*, Father
Olmedo.

MOTECUHZOMA

I don't need his instructions. Our gods have
always been good to us. They give us water
and food, cool rain and rich harvests. They
give us silence, and song. I wish to die the
man that I am.

EXTERIOR. SPANISH QUARTERS, MOTECUHZO-
MA'S COURTYARD. DUSK.

Beautiful Malinche is alone in the captive emperor's garden,
picking flowers, softly cooing a tune. Tiny hummingbirds
hover and flitter about her.

MALINCHE
Little flower, little flower, I am flowering
too / Pluck me, pluck me, whoever may wish
/ For alone, by myself, I will not move –

Motecuhzoma has walked up to her from behind. He startles
her, catching her off guard.

MOTECUHZOMA
It's said that sorrow comes out through
song when one can't cry –

Malinche, clearly uncomfortable with this, tries to cut off
any soulful probing, but only makes things worse.

MALINCHE
I wasn't stealing your flowers – they're for
you.

MOTECUHZOMA
They needn't be picked for me to know that.

Motecuhzoma steps even closer to her.

MOTECUHZOMA
May I have a word with you, Malinche?
Which you'll keep to yourself, as will I?
Just the two of us, alone, without your
master this time?

Malinche hesitates for several seconds, then nods her assent.

MOTECUHZOMA
Woman, you are an *Aztec*. Why have you
been so mean to your people? Why have
you sided with those who are not us?
Why can't you return to your own?

MALINCHE
I am with those who love me most. And my
lord –

MOTECUHZOMA
– only uses you.

MALINCHE
No. That's not true. Only *I* know who he
really is. There is no one kinder and more
loving than he.

MOTECUHZOMA
But he will forever remain a stranger to you.
Were you not born and raised here? Didn't
you play with your sisters and your
brothers? Didn't your mother sing to you?

Malinche tries to appear unmoved. Yet the tears welling in
her eyes betray her.

MALINCHE
I – I don't remember. I don't remember
anything.

Clutching a few of the flowers close to her heart, muting her
sobs, she exits abruptly. Alarmed guards with loaded arms
instantly encircle Motecuhzoma, who stands amid fallen
flowers watching Malinche rush off.

EXTERIOR. LAKESIDE. EVENING.

Geronimo de Aguilar wades into the water of the lake.
Rustling reeds, a small rock. He has spotted a very large
frog, sitting on the rock.

P.O.V. AGUILAR: CLOSE-UP OF VIGILANT FROG
STARING BACK AT HIM.

Footsteps. A hushed sob. Aguilar slowly turns away from the frog. He slips behind a cluster of reeds to see who the person is.

P.O.V. AGUILAR: CLOSE-UP OF TEARFUL MAL-INCHE WALKS TO THE WATER'S EDGE.

All of a sudden Malinche realizes she's being watched. She spots Aguilar, still standing knee-deep in the water, amid the reeds.

> AGUILAR
> Don't be frightened – it's me, Aguilar.

Malinche suppresses her last whimper.

> MALINCHE
> It's quite windy. Something's blown into my
> eye.

She quickly wipes a tear from her cheek.

> AGUILAR
> It must have been quite a sad wind. You
> know, Malinche, I saw those tears of yours.
> There's no need to hide them. But I never
> thought I would see you like this.

> MALINCHE
> It's not for you or anyone to see.

Aguilar wades out of the water and steps over to her.

> AGUILAR
> Don't feel ashamed that I saw you. Other-
> wise I would have always thought of your
> heart as a stone that couldn't be moved.

Malinche smiles to hear this. In his warm and earnest presence, she lowers her guard.

> MALINCHE
> Oh, it can be moved, but the time must be right.

> AGUILAR
> What do you mean?

> MALINCHE
> You know, before any one of you arrived, one of the temples here burned down. Nobody was prepared for this. Months passed before Motecuhzoma ordered that it be rebuilt with stone cut from a quarry not far from the city. When they came with their tools and coils of rope and prepared to move the first stone, it would not move, nor did it give any sign of wanting to. Then the immovable stone spoke: "Poor fools, why are you even trying? Haven't I told you you won't reach the city? It's taken you much too long to make up your minds…"

She realizes that she's somehow lost herself in the story.

> MALINCHE
> Goodness. Why am I telling you all of this? You know, I guess sometimes I behave like a little girl.

> AGUILAR
> You should be more like that. Everyone's afraid of you. You are the only Aztec who likes the Spaniards.

MALINCHE
Just one in particular. And you are the only
Spaniard who likes the Aztecs.

AGUILAR
Imagine if it had been me instead of the
captain to fall in love with you. And the
child we would bear –

MALINCHE
For heaven's sake, no! Anything but that!

He laughs. Only after a while does she join in, laughing like
a young girl. Both suddenly stop as they hear the clinking
and clanking of an armored Spanish sentry approach. He
is dressed head to toe in iron; curiously, even his visor is
down. Into the water he wades, rips out a long dry reed
and lowers it under his armor down his back. Fervently the
weird creature scratches at an itch he cannot reach, with
ever more urgent verve.

EXTERIOR. SPANISH QUARTERS, ROOF. DAY.

Motecuhzoma and Nezahualpilli, calm and contemplative,
walk across the palace roof. Among the Spanish guards
posted all around, two marksmen keep the Aztec ruler in
their sights, their cocked muskets aimed at him wherever
he goes.

In the square below, Aztec guards watch over Spanish guards.

NEZAHUALPILLI
Don't let them fool you. You hold Council
meetings here, you keep your women here,
the court ceremonies are strictly observed,
you give banquets, you even have your
jesters here – yet none of it's real. It's all just a
farce. You are like a man walking in his sleep,
my lord – a man who cannot be awakened.

MOTECUHZOMA
How can you say that. Aren't all of my
commands obeyed?

NEZAHUALPILLI
Does the Master of Malinche obey them?

MOTECUHZOMA
He's a different sort of creature.

NEZAHUALPILLI
He's a human being, and he intends to
destroy us. How often must I repeat this?

The two men walk on in silence. Then Nezahualpilli stops.

NEZAHUALPILLI
We can't go on like this. I, your vassal, King
of Texcoco, Nezahualpilli, challenge you to
a Divine Judgement. I call for a sacred
contest, on the ball court. If my side wins,
my view prevails. If your side wins, the
strangers are gods no humans can vanquish.

MOTECUHZOMA
I accept the challenge. But don't let yourself
be deceived by the strangers' bad behavior.
Gods are never saints. Wasn't our god Quetzalcoatl a drunkard, who even made his own
sister pregnant?

EXTERIOR. BALL COURT. DAY.

The modestly-sized playing field is equally divided for two
teams of four players. It is bordered on both sides by sloping walls, with a stone ring jutting from the vertical part of
the walls higher up.

(The object of the game is to pass a heavy, solid rubber ball through one of the two rings. The players may move the ball only with their hips and knees, which is why they protect their knees and mid-sections with leather pads.)

A few Aztecs silently attend as spectators. They seem to know what the stakes of this particular contest are.

Motecuhzoma and Cortés sit together on canopied seats. To Motecuhzoma's side is Nezahualpilli, to Cortés' side is Malinche. They watch the game, already in progress, and see the Aztec players vying for the ball.

Taking a cue from Motecuhzoma, one of Cortés' servants hands him a ball. Cortés is surprised by its weight. He bounces it once.

> CORTÉS (*Spanish*)
> Many things from this land will find a home
> in my country. Corn, turkeys, potatoes,
> tobacco –

> MOTECUHZOMA
> Yes, above all tobacco. It clears the head and
> makes you healthy.

> CORTÉS (*Spanish*)
> But I can't imagine games being played any-
> where else with balls like this made of gum.

> MOTECUHZOMA
> We call that gum "chicles." It comes from
> trees that weep. You can chew it as well.

He has one of the servants give Cortés a piece of chewing gum, then gestures in a sign language to him: put it in your mouth, chew it. Cortés does.

CLOSE-UP: CORTÉS, CHEWING, EXTENDS A STRING OF GUM IN WONDER.

CORTÉS (*Spanish*)
Now what's the point of this game? Tell me.

Never taking his eyes off the game, Motecuhzoma briefly replies, trying to downplay the actual significance of this event.

MOTECUHZOMA
It's just a game and no more.

Now we observe the contest more closely. The wild play is spirited and rough.

MED. CLOSE-UP: THE BALL SLAMS AGAINST THE STONE RING ONCE, TWICE.

Nezahualpilli's players manage to rebound the ball and suddenly bounce it off hips and knees up and through the ring.

This is the decisive move. The previously mute spectators now leap to their feet with a loud cry. The Spanish guards, thinking that any second the Aztecs will try to liberate their emperor, point their swords at Motecuhzoma.

EXTERIOR. SPANISH QUARTERS, MOTECUHZO-MA'S GARDEN. DUSK.

The captive ruler in his darkening garden. With him, aged Nezahualpilli. Motecuhzoma is bent over the blossoms of a fragrant shrub, never changing his pose.

Nezahualpilli paces back and force with the powerful steps of an energetic young man.

NEZAHUALPILLI
But my team *won*. How can you refuse to
accept this divine judgement?

CLOSE-UP: MOTECUHZOMA, ENTRANCED BY A
BLOSSOM, DOES NOT REPLY.

NEZAHUALPILLI
What will it take to convince you?

Motecuhzoma takes a deep breath to suck in the aroma of
a blossom.

NEZAHUALPILLI
Let me propose a wager: I'll bet my
kingdom...

MOTECUHZOMA
Against mine?

NEZAHUALPILLI
No. All you have to bet is a turkey. I'll bet
my kingdom against a turkey – against one
single turkey – that those alien creatures
are humans. In fact, they're men who are
plotting our destruction.

Contemplative Motecuhzoma finally turns to Nezahualpilli.

MOTECUHZOMA
Why a turkey? As king I have already bet
my life. Perhaps we can win back the Aztec
woman who came with them. You know, I
have been told we have figured out her past.

INTERIOR. SPANISH QUARTERS, MOTECUHZO-
MA'S ROOM. DAY.

Motecuhzoma on his throne. Only Cuitlahuac and Malinche are present. As Spanish guards pace back and forth
outside the doorway, Motecuzoma rises and approaches
Malinche.

MOTECUHZOMA
You do know why I asked you to come here.

Malinche hesitates. She senses something.

MALINCHE
Only what your brother just told me.

MOTECUHZOMA
I want you to tell me about your childhood.

She falls silent. For once, Malinche seems to be unsure of
herself.

MALINCHE
I – I don't remember being a child.

MOTECUHZOMA
So I suppose you don't remember your
mother?

MALINCHE
Yes, of course – I did have a mother.

MOTECUHZOMA
You *did*? But she's alive, you know. She's
here.

Lightning-struck, Malinche is unprepared for this. A few
seconds pass before she hardens again into the woman we
have come to know.

MALINCHE
Your brother lied to me. He said I was to
receive an important message.

Motecuhzoma makes a slight hand signal towards the
guarded door.

MOTECUHZOMA
And so you shall. Presently.

A woman of fifty is ushered into the room by a court
official. She freezes, rooted to the spot, trembling.

All eyes turn to her. Malinche is utterly stunned. The
woman tries to say something, but she can't. She begins to
rush toward her daughter, but after two halting steps she
throws herself to the ground. At the very same instant
Malinche, who had also stepped forward, stops suddenly.

Motecuhzoma confronts Malinche, face to face.

MOTECUHZOMA
You are a daughter of a great ruler to the
south. Don't you know that?

MALINCHE
I don't remember.

MOTECUHZOMA
You were six years old when your father died
and your mother remarried. Is that not so?

MALINCHE
I do not wish to remember.

Now Motecuhzoma turns to Malinche's mother, lying on
the floor.

MOTECUHZOMA
And when you bore a son for your new
husband, you had the odious notion to rob
your daughter of her rightful inheritance.
You pretended she had died, then buried the
child of a slave instead and performed the
obsequies in mock sorrow. Was that not so?

MOTHER
Lord, please –

Motecuhzoma thunders at her.

MOTECUHZOMA
Was that not so?

MOTHER
Yes, that was so. Kill me and say no more.

MOTECUHZOMA
And then you sold your own daughter to
itinerant traders!

CUITLAHUAC
You turned her into a lowly slave!

The woman on the floor remains mute. Malinche, who had
been restraining herself, now starts weeping convulsively.
Her sobs are touching because they occur in total silence.
A pause. Stillness.

Motecuhzoma turns to Malinche and speaks in a soft, completely changed tone.

MOTECUHZOMA
Shall we turn this woman over to you – or
do we kill her? Or shall we restore you to
your true name and rightful domain?

MALINCHE

I shall stay where I am and who I have
become. I'll be a much greater ruler without
you. I ask that you spare my mother. Do
not kill her.

MOTECUHZOMA

As you wish. But I want you to answer me:
why won't you return to your people?

Malinche wipes away her tears. She is suddenly quite clear
and decisive again.

MALINCHE

I love my lord. I love that man. He is my
god and savior. You see, only he truly
honors me.

MOTECUHZOMA

But –

MALINCHE

Can't you see I'm *pregnant*? Soon I shall
bear him a *child.*

Because she wears her usual, loosely-hanging garment, we
cannot discern that Malinche is pregnant. But we see by her
face that she's changed.

No one says another word.

EXTERIOR. CITY OF MEXICO-TENOCHTITLAN.
TWILIGHT.

A view over the city and lake. An oppressive calm in the
half-light has overcome the capital. We can make out the
Aztec warriors lying motionless at their posts. Across from
them, the Spaniards wait in tense anticipation at Axacayatl's
palace.

From the apex of the Great Pyramid come the slow pounding thuds of the drum. The first bats to appear sketch perplexed patterns on the darkening sky.

INTERIOR. SPANISH QUARTERS, MOTECUHZOMA'S ROOM. NIGHT.

A portable screen in front of Motecuhzoma's mat shields him from the eyes of the women in the room while he dines. From behind the partition his hand extends to receive bowls of food. Goblets are refilled as a flautist entertains the concealed man.

Some agitation at the door. The Spanish guards admit Cuauhtemoc.

> CUAUHTEMOC
> Forgive me, my lord.

The flute player interrupts his melody. Motecuhzoma has recognized the voice.

> MOTECUHZOMA (O.S.)
> Come closer, Cuauhtemoc. Speak to me.

Cuauhtemoc does as he's been told. His tone is hushed.

> CUAUHTEMOC (low)
> More strangers have landed at the coast.
> There are many of them – eleven times one
> hundred men, with many more deer. Our
> spies report that these men are very angry
> with the Master of Malinche. He's not what
> he says he is. He's not an emissary of any
> great lord. He's an outlaw, representing no
> one but himself. This huge army is far great-
> er than his, and their sole purpose in coming
> is to find the Master of Malinche and hang
> him from a tree.

MOTECUHZOMA (*O.S.*)
Remove the screen. And the food.

The attendants immediately obey his command, revealing Motecuhzoma, with numerous bowls of food around him. He has hardly touched any of it. A woman carefully pours water over his outstretched hands, another holds a basin beneath them, a third hands him a cloth to dry them. They promptly withdraw as the sovereign dries his hands. He cannot hide his surprise.

MOTECUHZOMA
Please continue, Cuauhtemoc.

CUAUHTEMOC
They are searching for him, and have asked where he can be found.

MOTECUHZOMA
Why is this? How did it come about?

CUAUHTEMOC
The Master of Malinche has betrayed his lord.

Motecuhzoma's stern countenance softens with encouragement.

MOTECUHZOMA
At last, our darkness ends.

For the first time we see this solemn man smile.

EXTERIOR. SPANISH QUARTERS, INNER COURTYARD. MORNING.

Excitement in the large inner courtyard. A hundred Spanish troops are ready to march. Twelve horsemen have mounted their steeds; the tethers for towing several light cannons are taut. Rations are distributed, gunpowder dispensed, bulging luggage lashed. In a state of alert, the Spanish guards on the roof surround the courtyard.

Cortés has his top officers around him; amid all this agitation he stays perfectly composed. He issues orders to Alvarado, who never strays from his side.

Motecuhzoma and his Crown Council are led into the courtyard by a sizable body of Spanish guards. Malinche enters with them. She stops at Cortés' shoulder.

> CORTÉS (*Spanish*)
> I presume you have learned of the arrival of
> my friends.

> MOTECUHZOMA
> We have heard about it. Why have they
> come?

> CORTÉS (*Spanish*)
> They have heard of the splendor of this city.
> They have come to honor me. And you.

> MALINCHE
> And there'll be many, many more to follow.

> CORTÉS (*Spanish*)
> I need two hundred porters. I'm eager to
> take a few of my men to the coast, to
> welcome my brethren.

Motecuhzoma sees through this, but hides it well. Cuauhtemoc is itching to say something. Malinche notices this.

> MALINCHE
> Prince?

CUAUHTEMOC
May I have a moment with my uncle alone?

When Malinche passes this on to Cortés, he nods his
assent as amiably as he can. Motecuhzoma steps aside with
Cuauhtemoc.

CUAUHTEMOC (*low*)
My lord, let's build a silver bridge for our
enemy. Give the Master of Malinche the
porters and make his way passable – it will
be his undoing. He and his men are about
to march to their own destruction. And we
will wipe out the ones who stay behind.

MOTECUHZOMA (*low*)
You are right, Cuauhtemoc. And you have
been right all along. But I have realized this
much too late. It's clear to me that you are
the one who shall carry on for me, who
shall see our people through this nightmare.

Now Motecuzoma walks directly over to Cortés.

MOTECUHZOMA
Master of Malinche, the porters will be ready
in one hour.

CORTÉS (*Spanish*)
That's very kind of you. How can I ever
thank you, my brother –

Cortés grabs Alvarado by the arm and draws him aside.
Malinche takes her cue.

MALINCHE
My master will return in a few days. His
brother Tonatiuh, The Sun, will command
those who stay behind.

Motecuhzoma feigns regret.

MOTECUHZOMA
Master of Malinche, in two days' time we
must celebrate our Festival of Youth. The
calendar orders us to do so once each year.
Do we have to celebrate without you?

Listening to Malinche's translation, Cortés' awareness
quickens. He suspects a trap. They confer confidentially.

CORTÉS (*Spanish*)
Will they be armed?

MALINCHE (*Spanish*)
They'll dance for two days and two nights.
And they're not allowed to be armed.

This satisfies Cortés. He embraces and kisses his prisoner.

EXTERIOR. CAUSEWAY. DAY.

Cortés leaves the city with a third of the Spanish force and
commences making his way down the southern causeway.
No spectators, no canoes on the lake. For a moment, the
City of Mexico's heart has stopped beating.

Cortés' standard bearer proceeds ahead of him, but there's
no other pomp. The Aztec porters are the formation's rear
guard. The departure takes place hastily.

EXTERIOR. ROOF OF SPANISH QUARTERS. DAY.

Red Alert conditions ensue for the Spanish soldiers still
on the roof. An uneasy calm has taken hold; the Spaniards
clearly no longer feel secure.

Motecuhzoma is with Cuauhtemoc on the roof watching Cortés' troops disappear into the distance. The emperor's legs are shackled with irons, which Alvarado must have clamped on him as soon as Cortés left, and he can only move in small steps.

CUAUHTEMOC
We mustn't lose any time.

MOTECUHZOMA
Humans can't change the calendar. First the
festival must take place.

There is something urgent in Cuauhtemoc's tone of voice.

CUAUHTEMOC
This is our chance to act – we can attack
tonight. Let's not waste any time.

MOTECUHZOMA
Cuauhtemoc, I have full confidence in you.
But you must learn to understand: Time
does not occur to a king.

EXTERIOR. TENOCHTITLAN, CENTRAL SQUARE.
DAY.

The main square is filled with dancers, bronze bodies bare but for loincloths, twirling and stomping to the sound of drums, conch shells and flutes. The festival's been long underway: the dancers are soaked with sweat, some exhausted ones having swooned to the ground.

Priests with incense, Aztec spectators, a few armed Spanish soldiers. An armistice of sorts seems to be in effect for the length of the festival.

Alvarado casually strolls in with a group of his men, pausing by one of the entrances to the square like an ordinary onlooker. Bored Spanish soldiers saunter in and linger at the other three entrances.

A few scattered Aztecs take note of the newcomers: something isn't right. Just then, several more Spaniards appear beside Alvarado; they resolutely make their way toward the middle of the square. The atmosphere gets edgy.

Upon the sudden blast from a musket the Spaniards storm forth. Only the exits are guarded. A terrifying massacre erupts. First the Spaniards assault the drummer and the music stops. Screams. Panic. The defenseless Aztecs attempting to flee are lanced by Spaniards at the exits.

Alvarado pushes his way into the heart of the fray, murdering everyone in his path. In no time, the square fills with the dead and dying.

EXTERIOR. CAUSEWAY. DAWN.

Returning on the southern causeway, Cortés approaches Tenochtitlan. We recognize his army by the standard, but the force is many times larger now than it was upon leaving. The eleven hundred or more are accompanied by a hundred or so horses, several cannons and assorted lethal weaponry.

The vanguard riding out front, led by Cortés, reach the island city's outer edge. No one anywhere: a city in a state of shock. And the big drum atop the Great Pyramid is mute.

EXTERIOR. TENOCHTITLAN, ROOFTOP. DAWN.

Two hidden warriors lie unmoving on the roof of a house, spying on the Spaniards as they enter the city beneath them.

INTERIOR. TENOCHTITLAN, ROOM IN HOUSE. DAWN.

A simple room with a mud floor. A woman and her four children crowd anxiously into a dark corner and listen to the hundreds of hooves stomping outside.

The father has punched a small hole in the front wall and peers through it as the hoofbeats pass worrisomely close, then the rumble of the rolling cannons.

EXTERIOR. LAKE OF MEXICO. DAWN.

Just before the Spanish army's rear guard marches from view into the city, canoes swarm onto the lake, heading straight for the empty causeway.

Once the canoes have reached bridges at two gaps in the span, the bridges are quickly removed. The operation seems well coordinated. The escape route for the Spaniards is now cut off.

INTERIOR. SPANISH QUARTERS, MOTECUHZO-MA'S ROOM. MORNING.

Motecuhzoma in leg irons, on his mat. The Spanish guards are in the middle of the room, some lounging disrespectful-ly in vulgar repose where the Crown Council normally sits during its sessions. Alvarado's command has changed things in Cortés' absence.

Cuauhtemoc is seated before the emperor between two sprawled Spaniards.

> CUAUTEMOC
> It's hard to believe. They came to hang him,
> and now they're marching with him. We
> have never seen such a master of persuasion.
> He casts a spell more potent than our

sorcerers. There are over a thousand of
them now.

MOTECUHZOMA
It isn't their number – it's their weapons
that we're defenseless against.

CUAUHTEMOC
As well as his military wizardry. You know,
the Master of Malinche attacked his brothers
at the coast while they slept. It was his one
hundred and fifty men against eleven hundred.
Their leader was wounded, and five of his men
shot. After that, the Master of Malinche spoke
to the others – just *spoke* to them – and they
immediately deserted to him. It's still hard to
believe.

MOTECUHZOMA
What can we do?

CUAUHTEMOC
We instantly stopped giving them food. And
we have taken the bridges away.

MOTECUHZOMA
Cuauhtemoc, are you already giving the
orders here?

CUAUHTEMOC
My father and I. We have to. Because from
the moment the dancers were slaughtered,
the spell was broken. No one will heed your
commands any more.

We hear Cortés' voice outside, roaring at Alvarado. He storms
into the room. Alvarado, Malinche and a few unfamiliar
Spanish faces crowd in after him. At Cortés' curt command
the guards spring to their feet and stand by the entrance.

Cortés himself lends a hand to help remove Motecuhzoma's leg irons. Then he embraces the unshackled man.

CORTÉS (*Spanish*)
You don't know how much it hurts me to see you this way.

MALINCHE
My lord suffers for you. He loves you like his dear brothers, who have just arrived from his homeland to help him, as you know.

MOTECUHZOMA
To *help* him or to *hang* him?

The emperor's stare drills right through her. He no longer holds anything back.

MOTECUHZOMA
What else will your lord demand of me now? Before he begins, tell him this: I do not wish to live any more, nor do I wish to listen.

Malinche translates this for Cortés. Brusquely he turns away, seething at being unable to count on his captive's support. The charade has ended. While leaving the room he starts roaring at Alvarado again.

Motecuhzoma and Cuauhtemoc suddenly find themselves alone, except for the guards at the portal. A momentary stillness.

CUAUHTEMOC
My lord?

MOTECUHZOMA
Look at me: there's nothing left of me but
my life. Just the man remains. Just him, and
his fear.

CUAUHTEMOC
Do you wish to be alone?

MOTECUHZOMA
I wish to see my children, the little ones.

EXTERIOR. SPANISH QUARTERS, MOTECUHZO-
MA'S GARDEN. DAY.

Motecuhzoma lies on his back on the stone tiles of his
little flowered courtyard, without sandals or insignia. Five
little children, ages one to four, are clambering and crawling
all over him, squealing with joy. The smallest one pisses in
his loincloth.

With his beloved burden well balanced on top of him,
Motecuzoma spreads his arms wide and looks up at the sky.

One last time we see Motecuhzoma smile.

EXTERIOR. SPANISH QUARTERS, ROOF. DAY.

Scores of Spanish defenders lie in position on the roof.
Cortés and Malinche escort Motecuhzoma, his neck in a
chained iron manacle, as Alvarado pushes and prods him
toward the balustrade like someone herding cattle.

The square below is filled with Aztec warriors. When their
shackled emperor appears, a furious roar of defiance erupts
from the teeming throng.

Cortés vehemently barks at Motecuhzoma.

CORTÉS (*Spanish*)
Do something! Tell them to withdraw! Tell
them we need food!

Motecuhzoma is totally aloof, his every speck of tension
shed. He calls out with a loud, firm voice to the volatile mob
of Aztecs below.

MOTECUHZOMA
Mexicans! Our flowers raise their heads in
the rain! Yet I, your emperor, wither and
fade. One last time I command you: care no
more for my safety, warriors – *ATTACK!*

A breathless silence below. Suddenly a scream from thousands and thousands of throats, then countless projectiles
hurled from the square pound the Spaniards like hailstones.

When two soldiers try to cover their hostage Motecuhzoma with their shields, he pushes them aside and steps
straight into the deadly deluge. A second too late, Alvarado
lunges to grab and save him, but Motecuzoma has already
been struck on the head by two rocks, and collapses.

In the chaos, Spaniards rescue the limp emperor and bear
him away.

INTERIOR. SPANISH QUARTERS, CORRIDOR. DAY.

The Spaniards have dumped the dying Motecuhzoma on
a corridor's floor. Only old Nezahualpilli is with him.
Armed Spaniards rush to and fro as Nezahualpilli tries to
cradle the emperor's bleeding head on his cloak. Motecuhzoma tries to speak, but he can barely whisper.

MOTECUHZOMA
I, as a singer, live on. My song will be heard.

Motecuhzoma's head slowly rolls to one side, and he gazes calmly at Nezahualpilli as death releases him.

EXTERIOR. TENOCHTITLAN, GREAT SQUARE. DAY.

The Aztecs' siege on the Spanish quarters has begun. Led by Cuauhtemoc, raging warriors swarm toward the main gate of Axacayatl's palace. A torrent of rocks, arrows and darts pours down on the Spaniards, who fire back from the doorway and roof with all their weaponry.

The Aztecs have learned at last how to react to cannons and gunfire. Once the wick is lit or the musket aimed, they throw themselves to the ground or swiftly zig-zag their way to safety.

EXTERIOR. SPANISH QUARTERS. DAY.

The surging Aztecs succeed in breaching the side wall of the palace. Shots, shrieks, smothering dust and fierce hand-to-hand combat atop the rubble.

Black smoke gushes from an upstairs window as Spaniards on the roof, under heavy attack, struggle to topple the ascending Aztecs' ladders being leaned against the building.

EXTERIOR. SPANISH QUARTERS, FRONT GATE. DAY.

A heated battle at the front entrance. The Aztecs seize a massive cannon from the Spaniards, dragging it off to the Great Square under intense fire. Suddenly they release the cannon and step back a bit. All eyes turn toward the front entrance.

P.O.V. AZTECS: SPANIARDS DUMP OUT MOTECU-ZOMA'S BODY LIKE TRASH.

A thousand-throated howl bursts from the crowd, resounding further and further through the city and out to its farthest edge.

INTERIOR. MOTECUHZOMA'S PALACE, THRONE ROOM. TWILIGHT.

Cuitlahuac now sits beneath a new canopy on a new wicker throne in the twilit chamber, wearing the regal insignia of power.

Before him are Cuauhtemoc, the Keeper of the House of Darkness, and some new faces. Elsewhere in the room are numerous high-ranking warriors. A lively debate is in progress.

                    CUAUHTEMOC
         We cannot allow them one second of rest.

                    CUITLAHUAC
         Aztecs do not fight at night, Cuauhtemoc.

                    CUAUHTEMOC
         But Venus is rising. Our power is peaking.

                    CUITLAHUAC
         They are still dangerous. We must be more
         cautious.

                    KEEPER
         Our losses have been appalling.

                    CUITLAHUAC
         I say we starve them out. They'll be finished
         in a couple of days.

This argument meets with general approval.

CUITLAHUAC
We Aztecs have but one task tonight:
to construct a funeral pyre worthy of
Motecuhzoma.

CUAUHTEMOC
I put my faith in our ascending star.

EXTERIOR. MOTECUHZOMA'S PALACE, ROOF.
EVENING.

Cuitlahuac and Cuauhtemoc stand at a rooftop balustrade.

Down below, the square is empty. The Aztec warriors have withdrawn.

To the left, climbing the steps of the Great Pyramid, a group of priests in black robes drag two Spanish prisoners toward the terrace above. One of the Spaniards struggles mightily, knowing he'll be sacrificed.

In the Spanish quarters beyond, the fire seems to have died, although black smoke keeps rising from there into the evening sky. At the front entrance, Spanish soldiers are feverishly erecting barricades.

Standing beside his father, Cuauhtemoc points skyward.

CUAUHTEMOC
Look. The evening star.

Past the city rooftops, the distant silhouettes of the two towering volcanoes, with Venus rising between them as the first visible star.

Cuitlahuac is in a euphoric mood.

CUITLAHUAC
In a few days we'll have liberated the City
of Mexico from all this terror. Look at them
building barricades – it won't do them any
good. Nothing will. Nothing they do can
stop us now.

CUAUHTEMOC
I don't trust the Master of Malinche as
much as I smell him. Everything he does is
a deception, Father. Everything he says is a
lie.

As the two men withdraw, Cuauhtemoc is somber, while
Cuitlahuac is confident and relieved.

CUITLAHUAC
So let him, my son. It doesn't matter.

EXTERIOR. SPANISH QUARTERS, FRONT ENTRANCE.
NIGHT.

Very slowly, very cautiously, the palace gate opens. Not a
sound. Nothing.

Suddenly, lit by the moon, armored Spanish horsemen
emerge in quadruple file, more and ever more. Only the
slightest clink and squeak of iron armor; the horses' hooves
are hardly audible.

CLOSE-UP: PADDED WITH RAGS, HORSES'
HOOVES HARDLY MAKE A SOUND.

CLOSE-UP: CANNON WHEELS, WRAPPED IN
RAGS, ROLLING NOISELESSLY.

CLOSE-UP: THE WEATHERED BOOTS OF INFAN-
TRYMEN STEALING INTO VIEW.

The Spanish infantrymen are attempting to escape with some sort of wooden structure, as yet unidentifiable.

A line of heavily-laden horses led by their reins, one after another. Mounted behind them is Cortés, surrounded by soldiers with drawn swords.

More and more Spaniards pour forth from the palace as the city sleeps. Not a word; scarcely a sound. Past the main square, the silhouettes of buildings slump against the sky like wakeless shadows.

EXTERIOR. TENOCHTITLAN PERIPHERY. NIGHT.

At the bottom of the embankment where the southern causeway begins, an Aztec woman is dipping water with an earthenware jug. Abruptly the matron stops and looks up.

P.O.V. WOMAN: FROM THE DARK CITY COMES A SILENT FORCE OF HORSEMEN.

She drops her jug. Instinctively she knows what's happening. The woman leaps to her feet and starts screaming.

> AZTEC WOMAN
> *MEXICANS! WARRIORS! HURRY!*
> *COME! THE WEIRD ONES ARE*
> *TRYING TO ESCAPE! THEY'RE*
> *TRYING TO ESCAPE!*

The horsemen in the vanguard gallop forth and overrun her with their lances. She falls dead into the water as drums suddenly begin to thunder from afar.

A deafening outcry rises from nearby buildings and spreads throughout the city.

Quickening their marching cadence with a start, the Spaniards flee.

EXTERIOR. CAUSEWAY. NIGHT.

The vanguard of horsemen has stopped by the first bridgeless gap in the cause-way. There is howling from the city and the dark lake on all sides. The Spaniards gaze upon a gaping space filled with water and moonlight.

The first Aztec canoes have reached both sides of the cause-way, where the horsemen already are under attack. Infantrymen have lowered the wooden structure over the breach in the span, and they proceed over this portable bridge as canoes swarm after them. The Spanish rear guard is set upon relentlessly by Aztec warriors on foot.

EXTERIOR. CAUSEWAY, SECOND GAP. NIGHT.

The Spaniards try to lay their wooden bridge over the second gap, but scores of canoes filled with warriors await them.

Warriors clamber onto the causeway and grab the nearly laid bridge. A pitched battle ensues amid screams and plummeting projectiles. The Spaniards answer with salvos blasted from their muskets.

In the mayhem we see defiant Aguilar breaking loose from the Spanish ranks to join the Aztecs. The horses go first as Aguilar and his fellow warriors wrest the bridge from the Spaniards.

With a heroic effort, Cuauhtemoc throws down a helmeted assailant, fighting hand-to-hand for control of the makeshift bridge.

At last the bridge crashes into the water with Spanish soldiers desperately clinging to it, as do a few Aztecs on the other side. The bridge drifts into the moonlit lake.

The stampeding Spaniards, not realizing their bridge is gone, push and shove themselves into the breach. When the first ones try to stop, the oncoming masses behind them who are unaware of the gap force them into the water. The lunging, kicking bodies quickly pile high. Horses tumble down with them. Screams, death, chaos.

Cortés crosses over the bridge of bodies and ruthlessly makes it to the other side amid furious hand-to-hand combat. Sopping wet, he flails away with his sword. Corpses of men and horses have so completely filled the gap that small contingents of Spanish troops struggle clumsily over them to catch up with their vanguard.

The fighting stops as abruptly as a rope snaps. Incredulous Aztecs gape from their canoes as their stunned brethren on the causeway yield in absolute amazement.

All of a sudden the screaming ends. Just a lone cry remains, so horrible it could come only from a beast.

P.O.V. AZTECS: ROARING ALVARADO, CHARGING FORTH WITH HIS LANCE.

Incredibly, his very long lance clutched horizontally before him, Alvarado reaches the breach at top speed, *impales* the wriggling mass of bodies, and pole vaults himself to safety.

Dumbstruck Aztecs watch several more Spaniards scramble after him before finally responding, and the brutal battle ensues.

EXTERIOR. LAKE OF MEXICO. MORNING.

The morning after the battle. A thick crush of canoes on both sides of the causeway. Rain begins to fall.

Near-naked Aztecs salvage weapons, luggage, corpses and loot from the lake, their long, hooked staves poking the bodies and pulling them up. Some dive into the water by the gap for helmets, crossbows, wooden chests and swords.

A dripping Spanish corpse is raised: Aguilar, in loincloth, drowned. His waterlogged body is hauled off in a hammock as several Aztecs hoist a dead horse from the water with heavy ropes.

Hundreds of dead Spaniards lie naked and pale in long rows on the causeway.

Further away, a row of dead horses. Blood is everywhere. With three quarters of its troops killed, the Spanish army has been devastated.

Aztecs busily untie burdens and saddlebags from dead horses. An enormous trove of gold bars is stacked higher and higher beside the bodies.

EXTERIOR. LAKE OF MEXICO, REEDS. MORNING.

MED. CLOSE-UP: A DEAD SPANISH SOLDIER FLOATING FACE DOWN IN LAKE

A few canoes drift among the reeds rimming the lake, retrieving bodies. Several penetrate the reeds looking for survivors. Calls echo, then a rustling of reeds and the blast of a musket.

EXTERIOR. END OF CAUSEWAY. MORNING.

Wounded Spanish survivors have regrouped where the causeway meets the mainland. Trembling horses, scattered gear, a few bloodied laggards wading ashore.

Only a handful of dugouts has pursued them this far, keeping a safe distance from the loaded cannon aimed at them. Curses, whistles; arrows fly through the air.

With Cortés standing on the causeway, leaning against his horse, among the survivors we see Malinche, Alvarado, Father Olmedo, youthful Bernal Díaz and some of the Spanish army's officers. Of the fifteen hundred Spanish troops, barely three hundred remain. All are sad, distressed, disconsolate; many of them ill, wounded, without boots, weak with hunger and thirst.

CLOSE-UP: CORTÉS GAZES THROUGH TEARS BACK AT THE CITY OF MEXICO.

EXTERIOR. LAKE OF MEXICO. SUNSET.

A calm has descended upon the water. The setting sun casts a pallid glow. A large, canopied barge moves across the serene lake.

EXTERIOR. BARGE ON LAKE. SUNSET.

Cuitlahuac sits on the royal seat beneath the canopy once occupied by Motecuhzoma listening to Cuauhtemoc, who has a bandaged head wound.

> CUAUHTEMOC
> We should have kept after them. Not one of
> them would be alive now.

> CUITLAHUAC
> Let them go. They were a bad dream, the
> sort that never returns. Tomorrow morning
> Mexico will waken to nothing but a distant
> echo.

The boat calmly moves on. The image slowly fades out.

EXTERIOR. FOREST IN THE MOUNTAINS. DAY.

Another landscape, another season. A long time has passed. It is winter. A sloping grove of mighty cedars, with deep snow blanketing the ground. The chopping of distant axes resounds. A falling tree crashes down, then another one.

Two Aztec scouts dressed in wool creep through the woods. They stop to look down below as axes ring out. They espy Indian woodsmen using Spanish saws to cut peeled trunks into planks. Three hard-worked horses pant visible puffs; a Spaniard counts planks stacked for transport.

EXTERIOR. MOTECUHZOMA'S PALACE, AVIARY. DAY.

A small tropical jungle housed in a fine netting of woven wicker. Flowers, whirring hummingbirds. Parrots, toucans, macaws and other exotic birds issue coos, ugly shrieks and urgent mating calls.

Cuitlahuac feeds a parrot some fruit as Cuauhtemoc looks on beside him.

                    CUAUHTEMOC
        I'm feeling a bit uneasy, Father.

Cuitlahuac is completely involved with the parrot.

                    CUITLAHUAC
        As always. That's nothing new.

                    CUAUHTEMOC
        I don't have as much confidence in what's
        going on as you.

                    CUITLAHUAC
        Be patient, son. You'll see.

                    CUAUHTEMOC
        You know, the strangers have damned the
        river in Tlaxcala, and have created a small
        lake. For *eight months* our spies in the

interior have been telling us that they're
building ships.

CUITLAHUAC

How else will they navigate the clouds and
winds and fog? On the backs of birds?

CUAUHTEMOC

What I cannot understand is why they're
testing the ships in a man-made pond, in the
middle of the mountains, in the middle of
our country, instead of somewhere on the
coast.

CUITLAHUAC

Because they're acting wisely. Inland their
work is sheltered from the harsh winds
and high seas they would encounter on the
coast. You mustn't let suspicion shape your
perception of things.

CUAUHTEMOC

But I just don't know what those half-dead
men are up to. And there's more, you know.
New ships have landed at the coast as well.
Big ones, with many of their brethren. If the
strangers are leaving, why are their numbers
increasing?

CUITLAHUAC

As tired as they are, and depleted, surely
they called for help. Just that and nothing
more.

EXTERIOR. PASS BETWEEN VOLCANOES. MORN-ING.

A clear day, with a distant view of the two volcanoes, their slopes glistening with snow. And something astonishing: an unending string of humanity is moving our way.

Flying towards them, we see Cortés' standard in front, then his horsemen walking their mounts, foot soldiers, marks-men, Indian allies pushing and tugging at cannons stuck in the snow. And something curious: thousands of Indian aux-iliary troops carrying planks, as well as cut and prefabricat-ed joinings and beams. The line of porters loses itself far in the distance.

On top of the snowy pass, four Aztec relay couriers see the procession below struggle towards them. They run away.

EXTERIOR. TENOCHTITLAN. DAY.

Paralyzing terror has spread over the city. Not a soul on the streets. Individual lamentations from inside the houses.

Corpses lie all over the streets, most wrapped in cloth shrouds, but some of them simply lying there naked.

We see two naked children covered with smallpox sores; flies swarm around their dead bodies. Dogs sniff at them.

INTERIOR. MOTECUHZOMA'S PALACE, THRONE ROOM. DAY.

Frightened servants cower in the throne room. Cuitlahuac lies outstretched on a mat beneath his feathered canopy, covered with woolen blankets. Women wipe his face with cool, damp cloths. Beside him is Cuauhtemoc.

CLOSE-UP: CUITLAHUAC'S RED, SWOLLEN FACE,
DISFIGURED BY SMALLPOX.

He is in considerable pain. A nurse carefully lifts the
blankets and touches a towel to his chest, which is covered
with smallpox sores.

> CUAUHTEMOC
> It's like their putrid breath, preceding them.
> We have never seen a disease like this. We
> are dying from it, all of us – but the strang-
> ers somehow are surviving it. The plague is
> faster than their deer; it's raced from town
> to town in the dead of night.

Cuitlahuac has trouble speaking.

> CUITLAHUAC
> How – How many of our people have died?
> I must go... see for... myself.

> CUAUHTEMOC
> We can't count them anymore. The shadows
> of night are shrouding them – as they have
> been shrouding you, dear Father.

> CUITLAHUAC
> Just... keep an eye... on the... Master of
> Malinche.

> CUAUHTEMOC
> I suspect he'll attack us sometime soon.
> He's encamped on the far shores of our lake,
> assembling his ships piece by piece. We have
> already attacked him from our canoes, but
> of course they were nothing against those
> fire irons of theirs. And then –

He hesitates to bring further bad news to the sick man.

> CUITLAHUAC
> *Speak* – tell me everything. Why… not? I'm
> *dying*, anyway.

> CUAUHTEMOC
> Well, only Xochimilco and Tacuba are still
> with us. All the others have gone over to the
> enemy.

EXTERIOR. WESTERN CAUSEWAY. DAY.

Parallel to the western causeway runs the aqueduct, where
Spanish soldiers are destroying the city's water lines.
A reinforced pipe elbow ruptures, and water gushes from it.

EXTERIOR. LAKE OF MEXICO. DAY.

Twelve gleaming Spanish brigantines sail toward us in a
floating phalanx as they begin to blockade the lake. Cortés'
standard waves atop the largest one.

Cortés stands at the helm of his flagship. He has assumed
command of the Spanish naval force.

Now the brigantines are attacked by a huge swarm of Aztec
canoes. The Spanish cannons bombard them, always blasting the canoes where they're most densely concentrated.

Explosions, smoke, death and destruction. The flagship
glides directly toward a canoe and overruns it.

Warriors swim for their lives, drowning everywhere, as
surviving canoes flee in retreat toward the city.

INTERIOR. MOTECUHZOMA'S PALACE, THRONE
ROOM. NIGHT.

None of the usual torches, only large basins filled with
live coals. In the waning light we can see women wrapping

Cutlahuac's body in its shroud. Laments abound amid widespread weeping.

High-ranking warriors have congregated here with high priests, along with Cuauhtemoc, the Keeper of the House of Darkness and old Nezahualpilli.

MED. CLOSE-UP: NEZAHUALPILLI TURNS TO A STONE-FACED CUAUHTEMOC.

> NEZAHUALPILLI
> You, Cuauhtemoc, youngest of the princes,
> oldest living heir, *you* are our only hope.

All eyes turn searchingly to him. Cuauhtemoc remains still for quite some time.

> CUAUHTEMOC
> *I shall fight unto death*, if only to save the
> memory of our great city, and to make sure
> that the glory of Mexico remains forever in
> the minds of men.

EXTERIOR. OUTSKIRTS OF TENOCHTITLAN. DAY.

The battle for Tenochtitian rages already with infernal fury. The noise hits us first: the pounding drone of drums, battle cries, the blasting of heavy artillery. The tumbling of walls.

Spanish troops have advanced over the causeways to positions outside the city. Systematically they shoot and bombard the buildings to ruins. Fires, devastation, people wounded and killed.

Cuauhtemoc launches a sortie at the vanguard of the ocelot warriors. Amid vicious hand-to-hand fighting, he's thrown back by musket blasts and rampaging horses.

EXTERIOR. OUTSKIRTS OF TENOCHTITLAN. DAY.

At the spot where Motecuzoma had welcomed Cortés to the city, all the houses have been razed, left in ruins. It is difficult to recognize the place.

Spaniards and their Indian allies have taken over and now work feverishly to fill the canals with the ruined houses' rubble, as columns of smoke rise distantly from fires in the city's center.

INTERIOR. MOTECUHZOMA'S PALACE. DAY.

A Council of War has been convened in the throne room. From far away we can hear the thunder of cannon fire.

Cuauhtemoc wears the spectacular, green-feathered cloak of the emperor, listening closely as the Keeper of the House of Darkness takes the floor.

> KEEPER
> Tonight just four of our canoes brought
> food over from the mainland. All the others
> were intercepted by the enemy's ships.
> Their fire irons have flattened the fringes of
> the city; now they can advance with their
> deer more easily. People are dying because
> their water's gone, so they're drinking foul
> water from the lake. There isn't one dog
> or lizard left – not even a *rat*. The warriors
> have started feeding on grass and weeds.
> And meanwhile more and more of us are
> dying from the enemy's plague.

Cuauhtemoc is completely tranquil and firm. He knows his fate. He is the one person present who holds his proud head high. The young emperor gestures for the ceremonial arrow, which is nearly as long as a spear.

CUAUHTEMOC
Aztecs, our fate rests in this sacred arrow.
It is time we dressed the Quetzal Owl, our
bravest warrior, in the garments of our god.

Attendants dress a tall, supremely powerful warrior in a be-
dazzling, feathered robe. Then Cuautemoc places the long
arrow in the warrior's hand

CUAUHTEMOC
The power of our gods resides in this finery.
Shoot the sacred arrow at our enemies, for it
is the Serpent of Fire, the Arrow that Pierces
the Fire. Shoot it at the invaders. Repel them
with the power of our gods. But, shoot it
straight, and far, for it must not fall to earth.
And if it wounds one or two of our foes, we
shall still have a little time left, and a chance
to defeat them.

The warrior, the Quetzal Owl, is fully absorbed in his mission.

QUETZAL OWL
I shall open the Quetzal feathers. When our
foes see me approach, they will quake, as if
a mountain fell on them.

CUAUHTEMOC
Terrify our enemies with it. Annihilate our
enemies with it. Let them behold it and
tremble.

EXTERIOR. TENOCHTITLAN, ROOF OF BUILD-
ING. DAY.

Accompanied by four Eagle Warriors, the Quetzal Owl
climbs onto the building's roof with the noise of battle below. Clouds of smoke come gushing up from

sudden fires, the structure being the focal point of bitter conflict.

The Quetzal Owl steps to the roof's edge and shakes his feathered outfit, then spreads his arms wide clutching bow and arrow. Instantly the Aztecs fall silent, and the Spaniards' noise also ebbs. Dumbfounded, the Spaniards follow the gaze of the Aztecs to the roof high above.

Atop the roof, the Quetzal Owl has placed the Irresistible Arrow in his bow. He aims and shoots.

MED. CLOSE-UP: THE OWL'S ARROW BOUNCES OFF A BENT SPANISH SHIELD.

The Quetzal Owl stands on the roof as if turned to stone. A lone Aztec cry of lamentation rises from below. Then, a totally unceremonious musketshot knocks the Quetzal Owl off his perch.

Screaming in terror, the Aztec defenders retreat hastily from the barricades.

EXTERIOR. TENOCHTITLAN, STREET. DAY.

Another city street. Some of the houses are on fire. A horde of Spanish horsemen comes galloping murderously through.

EXTERIOR. TENOCHTITLAN, THRONE ROOM. DAY.

The Council of War in the throne room. Some of the warriors in attendance are wounded. Cuauhtemoc watches his injured hand being dressed.

Nezahualpilli and the Keeper of the House of Darkness are present. The ministers have eschewed all matter and manner of court etiquette. Each of them looks Cuauhtemoc right in the eye.

NEZAHUALPILLI
Lord, we must keep you alive. You must be
given safe refuge somewhere.

CUAUHTEMOC
Never. I shall die fighting.

NEZAHUALPILLI
It's not *you* who's at issue now, it's
Mexico. The most we can hope for is that
you manage to find a way to reach the
mainland, unrecognized. We have to win
our allies back; it's all we can possibly do.
Only our ruler can do this. It's up to *you.*

KEEPER
Lots of canoes have been reaching the
shores with refugees. It would be no
problem at all to secretly smuggle you out.

This suggestion finds strong support. Everyone urges
Cuauhtemoc to accept it.

EXTERIOR. LAKE OF MEXICO. TWILIGHT.

The lake at dusk, rippled only by a gentle breeze. Boats
with women and children are fleeing the city. A few Spanish
brigantines cruise the waters in an intimidating manner. But
they leave the canoes unmolested.

One canoe, up close. It's plain, rather small. A single oarsman paddles it ahead slowly. In the dugout, in simple cloth-
ing, is Cuauhtemoc, the Keeper of the House of Darkness,
and Cuauhtemoc's fifteen-year-old wife. Still almost a child,
she possesses a majestic beauty.

A Spanish brigantine sails by. Curious Spaniards gawk at
the passengers in the canoe. A Tlaxcalan warrior aboard the
ship spots the disguised young emperor. The Indian points

and shouts, and quickly the Spaniards catch on to his discovery.

The brigantine turns in pursuit of the canoe. The dugout's oarsman starts rowing for his life, but the ship with the billowing sails soon apprehends it.

Suddenly Cuauhtemoc has his canoe head straight for the brigantine. He rises to his feet holding his spear and attacks, hurling it at the ship, only to see it rebound harmlessly off the tarred hull. Now Cuauhtemoc bobs in his boat, weaponless.

The Spaniards don't retaliate, but rather pull the canoe alongside them with a grappling hook. Cuauhtemoc stiffens momentarily and hesitates. Then the proud young emperor lets some Spanish soldiers take him captive.

EXTERIOR. LAKE OF MEXICO, CORTÉS' FLAGSHIP. DAY.

The brigantine holding captured Cuauhtemoc has been fastened to the flagship. Cuauhtemoc is led before the surprised Cortés, who signals for the ruler's shackles to be removed. Scarcely freed, he throws himself at Cortés and lunges for the captain's dagger.

CUAUHTEMOC
Kill me! Take your dagger and kill me!

Instantly he's manhandled by several guards.

CORTÉS/MALINCHE
It saddens me to see this splendid city
destroyed. I begged for peace and surrender
so many times. Why did you permit the
destruction of the city, with such loss of life
among your people and ours?

CUAUHTEMOC
Tell the captain that I have done my duty.
I have defended my city, my kingdom,
just as he would have defended *his* had I
attempted to take it from him. But I have
failed.

Cortés approaches the captive and looks him over for a moment.

Then, soothingly, Cortés pats Cuauhtemoc on the head.

CORTÉS (*Spanish*)
There, there –

MALINCHE
My lord loves you.

INTERIOR. LAKESIDE HOUSE. DAY.

In a single-level house with a hard mud floor, the Spaniards have set up a makeshift torture chamber.

Cuauhtemoc and the Keeper of the House of Darkness are side by side, tied to a crude wooden rack. Spanish soldiers busily shove basins of burning coals beneath their bare feet.

Cortés, Alvarado, the officers, Father Olmedo and a notary are present. Cortés is roughly clutching the young queen, Cuauhtemoc's wife, by her tiny wrist.

Malinche attends, with her sleeping infant cradled in her loving arms. Cortés addresses Cuauhtemoc with his sweetest of voices, as Malinche translates.

CORTÉS/MALINCHE
It has been wonderful sharing these
moments with you, however *indelicate* the
circumstances. Now, would I be incorrect

to presume that you have guarded our gold
with the greatest of care?

> MALINCHE
> So, Prince – *where's the gold?*

Cuauhtemoc is completely composed. He looks Cortés
hard in the eye without reply. Malinche now turns to the
Keeper.

> MALINCHE
> My master is getting a bit uncomfortable.
> I do suggest you tell me where he'll find the
> gold.

> KEEPER
> I don't know. Your allies have taken it.
> Every last bit.

> CORTÉS (*Spanish*)
> Surely you won't mind if I stimulate your
> memory a little.

> MALINCHE
> I'm warning you –

Cortés gestures for a captain, to whom he briefly mutters
something. What Malinche overhears is totally unexpected
and shocking. She turns to ice with a vacant look in her eyes.

Cortés takes her by the elbow and turns Malinche over to
the captain.

> CORTÉS (*Spanish*)
> This is my gift to you for exceptional
> service rendered in the name of our god and
> country. Take her for your wife, with my
> best wishes. Duty commands me to wed

this princess; my Mexican subjects would
accept no less.

Frozen, Malinche cannot speak. Cortés barks a snarling
command at her. Malinche haltingly tries to explain the
situation to Cuauhtemoc.

> MALINCHE
> Prince – Lord Cuauhtemoc – my master says
> that you will surely hold nothing against
> him for taking your wife, the princess, for
> his – wife. My master says, as ruler of
> Mexico he *must* take your wife. And I – I...

Malinche starts to weep. The baby in her arms wakes up and
starts wailing.

> MALINCHE
> And I shall be given to my master's captain
> as *his wife.*

CLOSE-UP: ANGUISHED MALINCHE'S WORLD IS
SUDDENLY TUMBLING DOWN.

Yet she rallies herself and regains her composure. Proudly
she lifts her head.

P.O.V. MALINCHE: SPANIARDS BEGIN BURNING
PRISONERS' FEET OVER FIRE.

CLOSE-UPS: THE KEEPER'S FACE, THEN CUAU-
HTEMOC'S, BOTH COMPOSED.

Abruptly the Keeper of the House of Darkness starts
screaming in agony.

Cuauhtemoc, ever proud and detached, continues lying there
with his feet to the fire. The brave, shackled young sovereign
makes no attempt to resist, and not a sound emits from his lips.

Nonplussed, Malinche stares at him with awe. She moves forward as if wanting to help him as the Keeper's agonized cries ensue.

CLOSE-UP: COMPASSIONATE MALINCHE GAZES INTO CUAUHTEMOC'S EYES.

CLOSE-UP: AT PEACE AND COMPOSED, CUAUHTEMOC GAZES BACK AT HÉR.

Her new husband, the Spanish captain, holds Malinche back.

>   MALINCHE
>   Prince, why don't you scream as well? Like
>   the other man?

CLOSE-UP: STILL TOTALLY COMPOSED, CUAUHTEMOC ANSWERS CASUALLY

>   CUAUHTEMOC
>   Am I not lying on a bed of roses?

The image swiftly fades.

EXTERIOR. CAUSEWAY. DAY.

The destroyed, burning city of Tenochtitlan. Black columns of smoke waft upward into the sky. Moving along the causeway is an endless stream of half-starved refugees.

An emaciated father in the chaotic procession is carrying his little boy on his shoulders. The child understands nothing, being too young to comprehend any of this. He laughs and rejoices, because it's so nice to be borne into the world.

FADE TO BLACK. FINAL CREDITS.